Also By Ken Renshaw

The Autobiography of a
Cambria House

A Friendly Guide to
Clairvoyance

? Crop Circles ?"

The Secret of Your Life Scrip

Science, Remote Viewing, and
ESP

The Trial of
The Psychic Spy

Is Clairvoyance
Possible?

A Novel By
Ken Renshaw

Copyright

Cover design by Heather UpChurch

To Joyce

My MUSE

Constellation Press
1790 Ogden Dr.
Cambria. CA 93428

The Trial of The Psychic Spy

Is Clairvoyance Possible?

1

WANDERING IN THE DESERT

I placed my emergency pack on the ground as a pillow in the shade under the wing of my sailplane and laid down for a nap. I closed my eyes and tried to recall the details of my flight. What had I done wrong to end up landing thirty miles away from the airport? I drifted off.

A terrible dream came. I was upside down in my car, hanging from my seatbelt. Tires squealed, and cars crashed, Some jolted me and increased the agony in my crushed left leg. Warm blood oozed. People shouted. Fire extinguishers belched and hissed. People pull on me. I scream. Consciousness fades.

The sound of the Pawnee tow plane jolted me from my dream. It was here to tow me back to CrystalSky. He saw me, cut his engine, landed, and taxied to me.

Dan turned off the engine, opened the cockpit side window and stepped out onto the wing. He was a man in his thirties, wearing jeans, a white t-shirt, and a cowboy hat over sound protecting earmuffs. He lifted one of his ear protectors, greeted me with a big smile. "Are you okay? You look freaked out."

"Yea, I had a weird dream. Must be something strange about this spot on the dry lake. I'm okay."

He nodded, drew the tow cable from the reel inside the Pawnee out to its one hundred and fifty-foot length, then handed me the end.

I hooked it to a hook in my sailplane nose.

In my cockpit, I went through my brief checklist. Thumbs-up! He started the engine, edged forward until the towline was taut, paused and then accelerated. In one-hundred feet I was airborne, flying. I followed the Pawnee as we climbed a few hundred feet and started a gentle turn toward CrystalSky. My hands loosened their hold on the control stick. This hot, sweaty, thirsty, and disappointing incident was over.

I feel depressed. That dream was from my subconscious. What is it trying to tell me? Is my life headed toward a big crash? Does this have anything to do with Raven? The questions faded as I turned my attention back to flying. The CrystalSky airport was only a few miles away.

Today, things had not gone according to plan. It was to be a simple sailplane-flying task, one I'd done many times before, suitable for the weak lift conditions of this warm Spring day. I'd planned to practice my flying skills by flying forty miles across the Mojave Desert from the CrystalSky Airport and return. I want to be ready for the day when the weather would be right too earn the International Diamond Soaring Award.

The air in the Mojave boils like water in a hot pan during still summer days. Streams of air bubbles rise from the surface and form into columns of rising air called thermals. Sometimes they join to form dust devils, little dirty tornados that suck up everything smaller than a person, often rising to fourteen thousand feet. I've seen pages of newspapers floating at ten thousand feet, migrating to wherever newspapers go to mate. Somehow, this area of the Mojave only simmered today.

The thermals disappeared as I flew over Rosamond Dry Lake, an expanse of dry silt five miles wide and five miles long. After I had landed near the western shore, within walking distance of the highway, I opened the canopy to take a big breath of the eighty-degree desert air.

I picked up my radio microphone and called, "CrystalSky this is King Romeo." My radio call sign "KR" is painted in large letters on my sailplane tail to identify me in soaring contests.

No answer! Out of radio range! Damn!

I was hot, disgusted. In the shade of the wing, I drank more water. My lips and face were salty from the sweat of the day.

A German-accented sailplane pilot called his ground crew on the radio. "Item Dog to base."

It was the call sign of Ingo Dorner, the world-famous pilot training for the World Soaring Championships.

I picked up the microphone and tried again.

"Any pilot, requesting a relay."

No answer. Damn! That pompous ass won't give me a relay.

Tried again.

No answer! Damn! Damn!

While cursing my luck, I walked toward the highway where the cell phone would work.

Does bringing Raven out here distract me from the concentration I need for flying? This is her fourth weekend in the desert with me. Has my flying been off when she is here?

I'd left this morning holding an unspoken disagreement with her. As I was getting ready to leave my desert home, uphill from the end of the CrystalSky airport runway, I told Raven, "I should be back in the early afternoon, I've planned an easy practice flight."

She studied me with a strange stare in her big brown eyes and said, "Maybe not. I'll fix a dinner we can eat any time if you get back late.

"What do you mean by 'maybe not?'"

Raven seemed to shrink. "I'm sorry I said anything. It is an intuitive thing I have. Sometimes I don't think before I express my intuition." I spoke in a lawyerly tone. "You know I have a scientific background and don't believe in any psychic fortune telling."

Raven stood up straight to her full five-foot-ten height and said, "How about this: there are only two cans of beer in the fridge. My intuition says we'll need more."

"Use my Porsche to go to that service station down on the main highway."

"Okay," she said changing back to her cheery self. "Have fun flying."

I recall that I was stiff as she gave me a kiss goodbye.

�֍

After a short trek across the desert, I saw a hill crowned by a big boulder. I climbed and took out my cell phone. *Two bars! Hooray!*

I called CrystalSky airport operations. Celia, the high school girl who worked at the airport, answered.

"Hi, Celia. This is Dave Willard. I need a retrieve from Rosamond Dry Lake."

"Hi, Dave. I don't have a tow plane available right now. The last student pilot has just started his lesson. He'll make four short flights. Then, Dan can tow you back. Where are you?"

"The west end of Rosamond Dry Lake."

"Dave, He'll be there in an hour or hour and a half."

"Thanks, goodbye."

I texted Raven, "I won't be home until 5:30."

I didn't talk to her. I didn't want to admit she was right.

As I walked back to my sailplane, I reminisced. The weekend had started well. I took Raven to a Black Tie reception at the Getty Villa antiquity museum in Malibu. She had looked fantastic in her black evening dress. She wore just the right make-up and had her hair in a fashionable bun.

"I want to look at the Cycladic and Greek vase display," she had said as we had cocktails and ate hors d'oeuvres in the atrium of the Villa. She steered me to one of the side galleries, filled with large, well-lit display cases containing clay-fired jugs, bowls, and other containers. She pointed to a large jar. "This is from the Cycladic civilization around 3,000 BCE, in the Aegean Sea. You can see only geometric carving on the jug."

Paul Jeffries, one of the senior partners in my law firm, and his young trophy wife, Elaine, joined us. I made introductions.

"Please continue with your description," said Paul. "Raven moved over to another case, leaned over, pointed, "This jar is from Athens, 500 BCE. It has black figures portraying Theseus battling the Minotaur. Jars in this area of the museum depict scenes from mythology."

Paul seemed more intent in looking down the front of Raven's dress than noticing the Minotaur.

"This one, over here, depicts Hercules, wearing the skin of the lion he slew, delivering a mortal blow to Kyknos."

Paul was very fascinated by skin.

"Interesting, thank you," Elaine, looked very threatened by the interest Paul was giving to the lecture, and to Raven. She led Paul away.

Raven looked concerned. "Did I say something wrong? Did I offend Elaine?"

"You offended her by being smart, in your twenties and having an athletic body. Elaine was threatened."

Raven looked concerned, "I know these are important people from your work. I hope to make a good impression."

"I think Elaine didn't like all the attention Paul paid to you. You did fine! Now finish telling me about the Minotaur."

A slight breeze came up as I continued to walk across the desert, sipping on my water.

Does contrast make good relationships? I'm a patent attorney dealing with hard scientific facts. She's a high school teacher, dealing with ideas. If only she'd leave this New Age mumbo jumbo alone.

I turned my attention back to flying my sailplane. The CrystalSky airport was only a few miles away.

2

WAS IT A VISION?

As we neared CrystalSky, Dan wiggled the wings of the tow plane to signal me to release the tow line. I released and entered the landing pattern. The sailplane rolled to the parking spot. I got out, stretched, and tied the wings down.

A cheery voice said, "Welcome back."

Raven handed me a tall, cool can of Coors. She wore tennis shoes, tan knee-length shorts, a white tank top, and a ball cap with her ponytail sticking out. I delighted in seeing she had nothing on under her top.

"I heard the tow plane and knew you were back." She stared at my face. "Is something the matter? Is landing in the desert that serious? Do I sense something else? Disagreement? Are we okay?"

"Something strange happened," I put my arm around her waist. Being near her made me feel better.

We walked the now deserted airfield to the path up the hill to my desert home. The airstrip was a mile long, paved for the middle half of its length: the rest was a sandstone colored swath bulldozed in the desert, strewn with small rocks, and bordered by chaparral and an occasional Joshua tree.

"Right after I texted you, I took a nap in the shade of the wing and had a horrifying dream about being in a car accident. It was more intense than a normal dream. I experienced emotions and pain as though I was in the wreck."

"Were you suffering from dehydration. It takes forty days and forty nights wandering in the desert to get mystical visions. You always seemed to be a quick study." She looked at me for a long time. "You're serious. This is upsetting you. I thought you didn't believe in visions and psychic stuff."

As we continued walking, I explained. "Dehydration: a logical explanation."

We walked for a while. I kept my distance while she glanced at me. After a long silence, she moved beside me and took my hand.

Her hand was warm and comforting.

Raven looked at me askance and said, "One of my teacher friend's uncle makes a living consulting with Hollywood studios forecasting audience's response to movies. He meditates and then gets a vision of people's emotions as they leave the theater after test screenings."

"That's Hollywood! Nothing is real there."

"Maybe you had a vision from somebody in a real car wreck."

I glared at her. Her big brown eyes were open wider than usual and her eyebrows raised. I knew she believed in this metaphysical stuff, but we both had been hesitant to talk about it.

I changed the subject. "I think I need another beer."

She linked her arm with mine. "Okay."

I walked the rest of the way home in silence. Coors therapy and affection made me better. We walked up onto my porch, and she steered me to a deck chair.

"Sit here big guy. Help is on the way."

She returned with a second Coors and said, "Dinner will be ready in a jiffy."

I drank and considered our relationship. *Her cheery nature makes her fun. But she makes me mad when she talks this mumbo-jumbo about psychic happenings. Mystical visions? I doubt that we could ever work the differences out.*

I gazed at the desert. *This place is my sanctuary. I shouldn't bring any upsetting company out here.*

My desert home is at 3,500 feet on the upslope of the San Gabriel Mountains, about a hundred miles north of L.A. This evening I could see fifty, or a hundred miles north across the Mojave Desert. On many days, I can see the blue outline of the southern end of the Sierra Nevada Mountain Range. Tonight, the desert breeze was stronger than normal. Thermals won't amount to much tomorrow.

Raven opened the screen door. "Let's have dinner on the back patio, out of the wind."

We ate our salads and had a glass of wine without too much conversation. I was still mulling over the events of the day. Raven was deep in thought.

As it grew dark, we heard a pack of coyotes yipping as they pursued prey: a jackrabbit running for his life. Then, it was quiet again.

I broke the awkward silence. "I love the evening sounds of the desert. Later, we may be treated to the sounds of the kangaroo rats shaking seeds off bushes. When I first came out here, I thought it was the sound of rattlesnakes and was afraid to go outside at night."

There was a long silence.

Raven spoke in a somewhat serious tone, "Come back! You're gone again. Get out of your vision."

"I'm sorry, I don't understand why this dream is affecting me so much. It is like an emotional hole of pain and confusion I keep falling into."

Raven paused a long time and observed my expression. She got up from the table, walked over, kissed me. "We should forget all this in the hot tub."

I awoke the next morning to see the sun glaring through the window.

I fell back in my bad dream. *I am straining to see out of the dirty, glare-fogged windshield. The big-rig truck in front of me swerves. I turn, but it's too late. It is rolling onto its side as I crash into it. The world tumbles. Then the sobbing image of my secretary, Zaza, appears.*

I smelled the coffee and heard Raven humming. I waited a minute to pull back out of the dream then walked to the kitchen. She was wearing one of my tee shirts that came to mid-thigh and chopping vegetables at the sink. I needed solace, so I hugged her from behind and kissed her on the cheek.

She shrugged her shoulders and pushed me away with her head. "Careful, I'll cut my finger or drop this knife on your toe. Get yourself a coffee."

I poured a cup of coffee, leaned my rear end against the counter, and glanced at Raven. She had her usual mischievous expression on her face. I wondered if she was putting something unusual in the omelet. She glanced back at me with a questioning look in her eyes. "I was expecting a much bigger smile this morning after last night."

"I apologize, As I woke I had another segment of the dream from yesterday on. You called it a vision. This dream was about what happened just before the crash. I'm over it now." I walked over and gave her a big kiss.

"That's more like it,. Let the dream go." She looked at me. "Let's change the subject.Is it going to be a good soaring day?"

"No. There's already a little breeze. Those high cirrus clouds are a bad sign. I'm distracted. I shouldn't fly without total concentration."

"Good, a woman I ran into on my walk was telling me about the Devil's Punchbowl in the hills not far from here. It's a State Park with an interesting energy, er, rock formations and has trails and self-guided tours." She showed me the State Park's page she had accessed on my iPad. "Pinyon pines, chipmunks, and California ground squirrels. A hike would be fun. They had some rain up there last week, and there may be wildflowers in bloom."

"Sounds good," *If you have seen one wildflower, you've seen them all.*

"I'll pack a lunch, clean up here and pack everything into the car while you put your sailplane away. We can leave for L.A. from the State Park. I know a great place on the way home for dinner."

As we ate breakfast, I could sense her excitement. "I love the desert. Desert tortoises, snakes, kangaroo rats bouncing around at night, coyotes yipping and howling. And then there are the wildflowers."

I felt better. "Snakes!" My arms shook in mock fear. Forget the visions.

She thrust my hat and a bottle of water into my hand and pushed me off the porch to get me started to the runway.

"This is fun," Raven exclaimed as we drove with the top down into the hills. She was wearing brief jeans shorts, a yellow tank top, and her ball cap. "Here, drink lots of water today. No more visions." She took a sip from a bottle of water and handed it to me. "Do you know what made the punchbowl?"

"The San Andreas fault. It runs along these mountains. The fault slips, the sandstone gets crunched and pushed up into jagged sky–pointing layers. Flash floods carve a deep valley down the middle. Voila, a Punchbowl.

"I've often flown over here in my sailplane but never visited on the ground. The Punchbowl is a reliable source of thermals. All that sandstone picks up the heat early in the day. See over there! That little wisp of a cloud must be over the Punchbowl from the first thermal of the day."

Before I could entertain thoughts of going back and breaking out my sailplane, she pointed at the map in her lap. "Turn left on that road up there. That sign says Tumbleweed Road. This is the way; we must not be far."

Soon, we were in the parking lot. We walked to the small weather-worn visitors center, went in, spent time looking at the exhibits of stuffed birds and animals, and bought a map. Outside, we descended the loop trail into the Punchbowl. It was a spectacular sight, a yellow sand, and gravel trail descending into a water-worn valley. Clumps of opportunistic shrubs and bushes grew in cracks. Raven stopped to examine the flora along the trail, named each plant, and touched the leaves and branches.

"I love Pinon Pines. They tower above all the rest of the shrubs and brush and seem to say to me, 'You can rise above any difficulty.'"

She turned to me and observed my faraway look. "Are you okay? Are we okay? You have gone away."

"Oh, sorry. I'm still trying to work out the logic of my dreams."

She looked toward the sky to avoid eye contact. "Many of my friends wouldn't think it was strange if you had a vision."

"In your world, it might be okay, but not in mine. I deal with scientific facts and logic."

"Here, drink more water." She handed me her bottle. "Why don't you take a nap in the shade of that big overhang while I continue to explore the trail? It goes on for about three-quarters of a mile—I'll be back in no time. The ranger said there were cactus plants in bloom up there, and I don't want to miss them. Just relax. Try meditating."

"Deal!" Not having any interest in desert blossoms. I stretched out on the ground in the shade of the big sandstone slab, shaped like a slice of tan layer cake hollowed out underneath by eons of flash floods. I put my hands behind my head, closed my eyes, and listened to the desert silence.

Enormous grief coming my way? What's going on?

Someone tickled me. "Wake up big boy," Raven stood over me. "Your loud snoring made the wildlife flee the canyon."

After shaking my head, sitting up, and rubbing my eyes, the grief faded.

"He's back?" Raven looked into my eyes.

As I looked into her eyes, my feeling shifted from grief to happiness.

She brightened. "I've been told there is something in this desert air called 'Funk-be-gone' that works every time. Come on, let's have our picnic."

She grabbed my hand, pulled me to my feet, and towed me up the path toward the visitors center. We went to the car, retrieved the cooler and Raven's wicker picnic basket, and walked to a picnic table in the shade of a Cottonwood tree.

"Isn't this great! Look at the view! That gentle breeze! Smell the sage!" Raven unpacked her wicker basket. She spread a red and white checkered tablecloth on the table, put out two blue plastic plates and silverware, produced two crystal flutes, which she filled with bottled water. As a final touch, placed a cut crystal vase in the center. She produced a cluster of daisies from a bag in the cooler., "Don't worry, Mr. Lawyer, I didn't pick these in the pristine raw desert. I picked these behind your house."

She then produced a bunch of grapes, cheese and crackers, and sandwiches, as she smiled.

"I was expecting a bag lunch."

She smoothed the tablecloth with her hand."Not for a beautiful setting like this."

She looks beautiful. Even with little makeup, she glows with inner exuberance. She puts off a soft energy.

We ate without saying much. She was taking in the view and the day.

After a while, I volunteered, "I had the intense emotion of my secretary crying over something.

Her beautiful brown eyes grew wide. "Was this related to the vision you had yesterday?"

" I'm not sure."

"Do you have a lot of bad dreams like these?"

"Never."

There was a long pause and then she said, "Let's talk about other kinds of dreams, like dreams of the future."

Clever segue.

She seemed to blush a little bit, "What dreams do you have for the future?"

"I don't have a big list. Everything is good. Oh, win this big patent case I've been working on for a year and work my way up the letterhead of the firm. I've yet to make that ultimate soaring flight. That kind of stuff. How about you?"

She looked a little embarrassed or disappointed. "I love to teach. That is my dream. Beverly Hills High is a great school. I like to explore new ideas, learn the secrets of life. It's a spiritual thing. Maybe, there's a vine covered cottage with a picket fence and a golden retriever out there somewhere."

Is she expecting me to have a dream of a relationship, marriage, or children?

She seemed to sense my sudden shift in mood. "I saw an Antelope Jack Rabbit today. They're bigger than a regular Jack Rabbit and have giant ears."

She looked at me. "You want to talk more about your dreams? Maybe they were visions of the future?"

"I'm not sure I believe in mystical visions that don't have a logical explanation Can you explanation them?"

She shrank away. "I've avoided talking about psychic things because the subject seems to upset you. I don't like to spoil our good times. My friend Elise, the one who had the uncle in Hollywood I told you about, has a Ph.D in psychology and likes to study strange things. Would you like to talk to her about your visions?"

"I guess I'm not ready for any of this yet, I'll find out about this later," My voice was formal. *This is making me mad.*

"I thought so." She looked away. "When you're ready."

"Thanks," *She has lost that beautiful glow.*

After a long and somewhat awkward silence, she folded her napkin, "Could we get back early. I could use more time to prepare for next week's teaching schedule. Tomorrow is another school day," Her voice was stern.

We finished our lunch without conversation, loaded the car and started the drive to LA. She slept most of the way.

After dropping Raven off at her apartment, I stopped for gas and walked into the station convenience store to get a cup of coffee. I saw a copy of the *Los Angeles Times* on the newsstand. The front page picture showed a big traffic pile-up around a collision on the 405 freeway. My heart sank. I bought the paper and read of the accident. *This is the same as in my vision! That's a relief. My vision—if that's what it was—was not of me having a wreck. Why am I even considering this? This Raven person is a bad influence.*

3

BEING A LAWYER

Monday traffic was normal on Santa Monica Boulevard, typical of L.A., everyone driving above the speed limit of forty-five with only a few car lengths between them while conducting important business on cell phones. I wanted to have silence this morning.

I turned into the driveway of the Century City building and drove down two floors to my parking spot. While unbuckling my seatbelt, I thought about my office and my schedule for today. Suddenly, a great sense of grief. came over me. *What is going on?*

I took the elevator to the lobby and joined the rush into the elevators to the upper floors. At my floor, the spacious lobby gleamed with chrome chairs and primary-colored cushions. Carolyn, the blond receptionist, looked like a professional model. Today, she wore a navy blue business suit with a white scarf tied around her neck.

"Good morning Mr. Willard!" Carolyn buzzed my secretary's phone to warn of my arrival. She gave me her "You're the most interesting person. Notice that I'm available" smile.

"Good morning!" I tried to feign interest in her implied offer. *Good. That sadness has gone away.* I walked past her down the hall to my office. Rodger, also a patent attorney and a close friend, shared the mahogany-walled suite.

Our secretary, Zaza, sat at a chrome and ebony desk between our offices. While staring at her and my grief grew. My mind flashed to Carolyn, and my grief disappeared. When I put my attention back on Zaza, the grief engulfed me. *She is the source of this terrible feeling! How can that be?*

Zaza Green, whose real name was Zahavia, was in her late forties, plump, with gray hair in the perm style she got married in and had worn ever since. Her skin was sallow and wrinkled as it would be for a pack-a-day smoker who had almost quit. A blue blouse exposed some of her abundant cleavage of the type no one wants to see. Zaza's manner ran from businesslike to covertly hostile, and I usually got the latter. Today she seemed to be on the verge of tears.

"What's the matter?" I asked.

"Rodger died!" She struggled to stop crying.

"What happened?" I was stunned beyond belief. "I talked to him just before we left the office Friday. He seemed fine."

She burst into tears. "His Ferrari was crushed by a big truck on the freeway. I saw the accident reported on the news. I didn't know it was Rodger until a relative called from his home this morning."

I handed Zaza a tissue she held over her nose and continued to wail.

"I'll be back soon." She headed for the women's room.

I walked into my office and dialed Rodger's home number. A man answered with a sad voice.

"This is Dave Willard from Rodger's office calling. I'm so sorry. How is Annie doing?"

The voice introduced himself as Annie's brother and said Annie was sleeping.

"Please tell her how sorry we all are at Bracken and Stevens. Let me know if there is anything we can do. Please call me anytime. Rodger and I shared the same office suite."

"Thank you," he replied. "I'll tell her you called."

Shocked, I sat in my office for a long time. *In my vision, I had sensed what Rodger had experienced crushed in his car! How could that be?*

Zaza buzzed me and said, "Patty, Bracken's secretary just called. She said Ms. Davis in the PR office would take over and handle sending flowers, and anything else appropriate for the memorial service. She'll also arrange for town cars for Annie to use and to pick people up at the airport. We don't have to take care of anything.

"Good!" I said. "Let's take the rest of the day off."

I wast a little better the next morning entering my office. When my attention turned to Zaza, deep grief washed over me.

My thoughts turned to Carolyn, and the grief went away. *I'll have to remember that.*

I went into my office, and started going through my email. *It is nice to be back into doing something orderly and logical.* After a while, Zaza buzzed my phone, "George Downey has arrived and is in the conference room."

"Okay." Carolyn charmed scheduled visitors and then showed them in. *I'm glad that Zaza didn't represent me.*

George is one of the technical experts we often use in our patent trials. He has two Ph.Ds and specializes in electromagnetic devices. Today he was, as usual, dressed in his scientist uniform; a tweed sports coat he wore in all seasons that did not quite match his slacks. Leather patches on the elbows, and a plastic pocket protector with several pens in the inside pocket completed his ensemble. He was tan with balding gray hair and intense blue eyes, and today, as usual, he looked serious.

We discussed some of the technical issues in the patent case I was working on and talked about how we would present the information in lay terms. As he was getting ready to leave, we began chatting about cell phones and where they worked and where they didn't.

"Last Sunday, in a quiet moment, I had a hazy vision of an accident on the 405. Later, I found out that my lawyer associate died in that accident at the same time. Do you have any idea how that happened?"

Oh-oh. I shouldn't have said that.. George looks like I stomped on his toe. His face is growing red. I hope he doesn't have a stroke.

George's back straightened."There is nothing in electromagnetic theory that would explain that."

"Electromagnetic theory?"

George grew stern. "Anything like a vision is against the laws of physics. For the cell phones, we were talking about, theory says that as you get farther from a cell tower, the signal or number of bars goes down exponentially. If you're one mile from a cell tower and you move to two miles away from it, the signal level drops by a factor of eight."

I know about searching for bars on my cell phone while walking in the desert.

George continued his lecture, "Two human bodies jammed together couldn't make enough electrical energy transmitted to be observable," George concluded with his usual logic. "Miles away? No way!"

My mind switched to Raven, our bodies jammed together and the energy we created.

It was obvious George was getting upset. I changed the subject. "What kind of cell phone would work best in the desert where there are few cell towers?"

George got madder. "That's why all that crazy stuff about ESP is pure ignorance, superstition, or the tricks of charlatans. It's all against the laws of physics. It doesn't happen except to people with limited critical thinking skills and a gullible imagination."

"Thanks, George." His eyes were beady, and he was fuming. I walked him to Carolyn to make sure he got his parking ticket validated. Carolyn did her shy act with her eyes lowered and chin down and chatted to attracted his attention.

"Goodbye, George. That was a productive meeting." I shook his hand and returned to my office.

I've got to learn to be careful not to mention ESP with scientific people like George. I'm sure he thinks less of me for broaching a metaphysical subject with him. Raven must be a bad influence.

When I got back to my office, Zaza said, "I forgot to ask, how was your weekend in the desert? Did Flopsy go with you?"

"Raven Corbin was with me."

"Flopsy, Popsey or Cottontail, I couldn't even keep your desert rabbits straight. Now there is a bird. Are flowers in order?"

I thought for a second. "Yes, that would be a good idea. Send her a bouquet of daisies or something cheerful like that. On the card say, 'for a delightful picnic.'"

Zaza replied with slight scorn, "Popey got roses. Give me this Raven's address.

4

BAD GOOD NEWS

After lunch, Zaza buzzed me. "Mr. Bracken wants to see you."

"Right now?"

"'At once' was what he said," replied Zaza with her sarcastic tone.

When I arrived at Phil Bracken's office his secretary, Patty, gave me a look that said something wonderful has happened. I walked into Phil's office. "First, I was sorry to hear of the loss of Rodger. PR is handling our obligations. But that isn't why I called you.

He left his chair to give me an enthusiastic handshake and a professional, polished smile. "Congratulations! They settled! Have a seat," he gestured to a chair. "I guess after they saw your witness list and the backgrounds of those witnesses, they caved. They met with Paul in our Washington office and offered a settlement. Paul talked to his friend Robert Sampson, the CEO at Genstem and he accepted their offer. We won! Here is the settlement."

He pushed a copy of the email across the desk. As I read it, I was stunned. It was more than expected.

"So, we don't have to go to trial." I was in a state of shock. A whole year's work evaporated.

"Don't worry," Phil said. "Paul and the Washington office will take it from here. Why don't you take a few days vacation? If they need anything, we can call you. Have Zaza keep Patty informed of where to contact you." He got up and shook my hand again. "Good work! Congratulations! We'll talk later. I have to leave for Detroit."

I walked back to my office still stunned. Actors need audiences, and trial lawyers need juries to thrive. Our law firm won. I lost.

Zaza greeted me with, "Patty told me the news. You're unemployed!"

Damn! Why did she have to put it like that? That is adding insult to injury.

"I'm going to the desert. You can call me out there."

"You forgot your briefcase," said Zaza.

In my apartment, I checked my voicemail and heard Raven's voice: "Thanks for the flowers. I called to thank you on your cell phone, but you didn't answer, and then tried your office. Your secretary said you had just left. She didn't know when you would be back. I asked whether you were on a business trip. All she said was 'No.' She sounded very abrupt. Is everything OK?"

That's Zaza. She can never pass along any good news. Raven must have called while I was in the parking garage.

I called her home phone and left a message, explaining they settled the case I had been working on for a year, Everything is fine. I'm taking a few days off in the desert.

Is this be the meaning of my life? I Produce boxes of legal briefs that get filed away in some dusty warehouse and fat checks that dissolve into insignificance in Big Pharma accounting systems. Maybe having Raven in my life is what I need.

I arrived at CrystalSky at dusk. The evening star was rising in the west.

Good evening, Hesperus!

Most people referred to the evening star as Venus. I prefer the Greek male version where Hesperus is the leader of the stars as they march into the evening sky. He has excellent organizational powers and gets the other stars to their places. I wonder how he feels having to do the same old thing night after night??

It was already chilly. I hurried into the house, put my bag in the bedroom, and went to the closet for a down jacket. Two hung in a plastic wardrobe bag. Mine was the lighter one of two. The warmer down jacket for guests bathed in the aroma of cedar chips and sage in the bottom of the bag, placed there to hide the scent of whoever had worn the jacket last, most recently, Raven.

Is this what I want out of life?

I shook the wardrobe bag to spread the chips.

In the kitchen, I poured myself a brandy, walked out onto the patio with the view of the desert, and sat in one of the white plastic chairs. I put my feet up on a table, rocked back and looked at the zillions of stars in the desert sky.

Damn, I'm unemployed, Rogers dead, and I'm lonely.

I called Raven. "Hi, Raven, I'm calling you from the desert. How are you doing?"

"Oh, thank you for the flowers. They are so beautiful, my favorite kind. They were here when I got home from school."

I wondered what Zaza had sent.

"How is the weather out there? I got your message about taking a few days off. Was finishing the case a bad thing? You sound down."

I won't tell her about how Roger's death and my vision.

"It is beautiful, cold, and clear. It's good to settle a case –at least for the client and the firm–but I won't get to go to trial. That's the fun of being a lawyer. I make dramatic speeches and take opponent counsel's witnesses apart on the stand. Now, I'll start with a new client and won't get to do my thing for a year."

"Will it be more scientific stuff?"

"Yes, that's what I do for a living."

"Any more visions?"

"No. This morning I learned the attorney I share an office suite with died in a freeway accident about the time of my first bad dream on the dry lake."

"Wow! That's heavy. Do you think your vision sensed what your office partner experienced?"

"I can't go there yet. I am still searching for a logical explanation. It's a lot to process." My voice had grown lawyerly-formal. Still, I ventured to ask, "Any chance you might like to visit the desert again this weekend?"

"I can't right now. End-of-school-year testing and grading, and my night school courses will keep me buried until the end of the term." She paused. "Someone's at the door. I have to go now. Say hello to the kangaroo rats for me. Goodbye."

My heart sank. I would have to start over in that department as well. Too bad. Raven was fun to be with unless she was talking nonsense about metaphysical things. No long-term future there. It was a good thing we had that conversation at the Punchbowl that showed me who she is.

We sat for a few minutes, just Hesperus and me, and watched his followers deploy. *Hesperus, does your life ever come apart?*

5

A NEW BEGINNING

The first light of dawn was just breaking when I made a cup of coffee, put on my parka, and walked into the desert to clear away the mind-fog.

It was cold. The cacti and sagebrush wore a fine coat of silver frost, glittering in the first rays of the dawn light. The sun came up. I felt the heat on my face. Frost evaporated. The new day was. My head cleared as I viewed a hundred miles of desert to the North. Sunlight on the dark buttes and distant mountains spread down from the peaks to the valleys.

Back from my walk, I had breakfast, read the New York Times, the Washington Post, and the L.A. Times on my iPad. The news didn't lift my spirits.

My cell phone rang. Raven, I hoped. I looked. It was Zaza.

"Vacation is over. Bracken wants to know whether you can meet with a new client tomorrow morning at nine o'clock."

"Sure. Who is the client?"

"They didn't tell me. Bracken's secretary, Patty, laughed when she called–like it was a joke–and said you would love this case. I hope this doesn't upsets your social plans."

"No problem. See you tomorrow."

I worried as I walked into the office lobby the next day. *Am I going to spend the next year with a client I hate or working on a patent for an unethical product?*

"Good morning Mr. Willard!" Carolyn gave me her usual 'How wonderful you are here, and I'm very available' smile.' I rolled my eyes and returned her smile.

Zaza looked grumpy as usual. "How was your long vacation?"

"A pleasant respite." I looked at Zaza. "Everything okay?"

She looked mournful. "Life goes on."

I walked into my office.

In a few minutes, Zaza's buzzed me on the intercom and announced, "They're here!"

I walked into the conference room and saw Phil Bracken with a very attractive woman.

"Dave Willard, meet Danae Hamilton."

Danae wore a navy blue suit with a red scarf. She was about five-foot-two, with a compact athletic look, about thirty years old, with brown eyes. Her streaked hair parted in the middle showed she spent time in an expensive hair salon. The white areas around the eyes that suggested she had been skiing.

She smiled with a flash of recognition in her eyes as she shook my hand. "Pleased to meet you, Mr. Willard," She reset to an icy stare. I knew I had been professionally 'made,' fully assessed, and judged.

"Pleased to meet you, Ms. Hamilton," I replied without losing eye contact. *She is one tough lady.*

Phil began, "Ms. Hamilton is an assistant to an old friend of mine, and a good client, Vince Colson, who has a venture capital firm in Palo Alto. He funded a foundation, the Colson Foundation, to support the investigation into paranormal phenomena and other pet projects. He wants us to take on a test case to try a county sheriff for negligence. It failed to use an available psychic resource and prevent the death of a lost child. Colson's Northern California attorneys have started proceedings in Rocky Butte County on behalf of the parents of the child. Ms. Hamilton has outlined the case. It is something Bracken and Stevens should take on. The timing of the case is perfect for you since your Gensten case settled."

Oh, no! More of this metaphysical nonsense, Why me?

I understand why Phil wants to take this on. I have heard Colton has a big case coming up in the next year.

Ms. Hamilton sensed my reaction, "Mr. Willard, I expect that this is somewhat far afield from your patent law subjects. Phil said that you were a master at presenting complicated scientific cases in terms that can be understood by lay juries."

I flinched. *Is Bracken trying to drive me out of the firm with this case. He says he appreciates my scientific integrity. Is he assigning this to me to make me quit? Has there been some screw-up of my last case?*

32

Danae made eye contact with me. "The Colson Foundation has sponsored research that will offer the basis for a scientific case. The challenge will be convincing a jury of a legitimate explanation for how the psychic could sense the whereabouts of a lost girl."

My heart sank. *I can see me presenting this to a jury.*

"Phil warned me that you might be skeptical. We consider that a plus. If you can convince yourself there is a basis for a man's clarvoyant ability, you can convince a jury."

Convincing myself is going be the hard part.

"I think I meet your requirements for lack of knowledge of psychic abilities,"

"Good. Are you be available to go to Palo Alto today to meet with Mr. Colson? He is scheduled to leave town tomorrow on a business trip. He's anxious for you to get started."

"Of course." *Oh boy! I get to go through airport security twice in one day.*

"Thank you, Phil." Danae shook Phil's hand. "I've confidence that we've made the right choice in asking your firm to represent us."

"Thank you for selecting Bracken and Stevens."

I motioned toward my office."I'll get my briefcase."

I waved at Zaza on the way out. "I'm going to Palo Alto–be back tomorrow."

Zaza couldn't resist: "She's a hot one! I saw her when she came in. What are Flopsey and the Raven going to think?"

"I'll see you tomorrow." I played it straight as always.

Danae was in the lobby texting. We took the elevator to the ground floor and got into a black chauffeured town car.

"Excuse me, I have to check in with my office." Danae continued texting on her iPhone. I took out my phone and reviewed my email.

I was surprised when the driver turned north on the 405 instead of south toward LAX. I didn't comment.

Soon, we were at the Van Nuyss airport, and the driver drove to a Learjet parked in front of one of the hangars. A lean, uniformed pilot with surfer-length blonde hair sticking out beneath his navy blue pilot's cap greeted us. I looked into the cockpit as we entered, and saw a female pilot, also in uniform, going through the preflight checklist.

The jet had six brown leather seats, two in the back and two facing each other separated by the aisle and two at a small table. The interior smelled of leather with a slight hint of jet fumes.

Danae motioned to one of the two brown leather seats at the table as I heard the engines start.

"Thanks, Ms. Hamilton."

We both fastened our seat belts as the jet began to taxi.

She smiled. "Make it Danae."

"Dave," I replied with a nod.

We both looked out the window as the jet paused before entering the runway and began the takeoff roll.

"Dave, you have dark tan for a person with your light skin. Are you a golfer?"

"No, I spend a lot of time in the desert. I have a sailplane."

"One of those things where they tow you up in the air, and then you glide down?"

"Yes, but sometimes we stay up for hours and fly cross-country. It's quite a sport,"

Danae stared at me for a second. "I get that there is something competitive about that."

Damn! How did I get a client who thinks she can read my mind.

"No, it's something I do alone,"

Danae stared at me again for a few seconds. "When you were in college, there was something competitive. Tennis?"

I was shocked. "Right! I was a varsity tennis player."

This is scary! What kind of lawyer-client relationship are we going to have?

"You will have to tell me about it sometime. Please excuse my delving into your past. The energy was strong, hard to resist."

"Your tan looks like someone who has just been skiing."

"Right, very observant. My partner and I were in Aspen for a week not long ago."

My partner? She might be gay.

"Her company has a condo there, so it's very convenient."

That's a relief. She is setting some ground rules for our relationship, taking gender out of the equation.

She made eye contact and leaned slightly toward me. "Have you had any personal experience with psychic phenomena?"

Here we go. We're starting the job interview. "My experiences are mostly from movies, television, and other fiction. I have a girl-friend who surprises me now and then with an intuition of things happening in the future. *That should give her my acknowledgment that I understand this is only a business relationship.*

"Good! A good clean slate to work with. Here is a book, a good starting point, written by Steve Manteo who is the psychic who was ignored by the Sheriff in our case. We'll get to the scientific part of the case later after you understand the phenomenon involved." She produced a hardbound book with a bright red cover and the title The Psychic Spy Who Never Left His Office.

What have I gotten myself into? I took the book. *Reading is a good way to kill the flight time to Palo Alto.*

I was incredulous as I read through the book. Steve Manteo had been an undergraduate at Stanford taking a lower division psychology course. One of their lab sections did a series of ESP experiments. At the start of a lab session, the instructor would walk to a place such as at the campus post office without announcing his destination. Students were asked to meditate and perceive the location. Steve was the only person in the class who identified all the locations

The class didn't know that the professor was doing both legitimate academic research and searching for candidates for a psychic spy program at SRI, the Stanford Research Institute. Steve was asked whether he would like a part-time job. Since Steve was working his way through school, he accepted the offer.

He worked part-time until he graduated in architecture, after which he went to work for one of the CIA's classified contractors. He worked on the CIA-sponsored program for twenty years, spending hours each day perceiving assigned cold-war psychic targets; the location, and activity of people of interest, or the nature of activities in buildings and factories in the Soviet Union.

I closed the book as I heard the jet's flaps go down in preparation for landing. *I wonder if this has anything to do with my vision of Roger's accident??*

Danae closed her laptop. "Amazing stuff isn't it? The psychic spy program continued for twenty years, without anybody hearing of it. The contractor Steve worked for had annual incremental funding from the CIA, which meant that every year someone in the CIA had to justify the program's effectiveness for it to continue."

I looked out the window as we descended to the Palo Alto airport, trying not to reveal my skepticism about this whole turn of events in my life. I mulled over what I had just read.

Another black town car waited by the hangar.

Colson Associates was in a modern but unassuming building, on a slight rise, in an office park surrounded by trees displaying their spring foliage.

A receptionist sitting at a modern glass table with a laptop looked up and greeted Danae. "Dr. Colson said to send you right in."

As we entered the conference room, a man of around fifty years old, medium height, slightly balding, salt and pepper hair, sitting in one of the overstuffed chairs, tapped a button on his laptop. He closed the lid, looked up, and walked over to us.

Danae said, "David Willard, meet Vince Colson." Vince Colson had a very relaxed demeanor. He wore a blue and white striped button-down shirt with no tie, khaki pants, and black, leather-topped running shoes. As we shook hands, I felt as though I was going through a security scanner at the airport. With one piercing look, he knew everything about me. I had been 'made' again.

"Is this the Foundation or the Venture Capital building?"

"The VC analysts occupy the building. Right now, Danae and I are the only Foundation employees."

I Looked at Vince. "Could you tell me a little about the Foundation?"

"Certainly." He motioned for us to sit down at the conference table. "I've enjoyed some business success because of what I call 'intuition.' I can read a lot of people by concentrating on them. Often, a feeling about the future of a venture someone is pitching turns out to be right."

My mind flashed to Raven. She seems to have some of those abilities.

"About a decade ago, a fellow appeared at my office saying he was a former member of a highly classified CIA psychic spy program that had been declassified. He claimed he had made a killing in the silver futures market, a fact I later verified from other sources. I learned about remote viewing, one of the spy-crafts the CIA used. Now, this ex-psychic spy was offering consulting services. I've used him to assess people and evaluate potential business ventures. He is good at what he does."

"The consultant is Steve Manteo." Danae pointed to the book she gave me. "His advice has been useful many times."

Vince nodded his head in agreement. "I want the Foundation to explore the general idea of remote viewing and clairvoyance."

"We've been funding academic research to understand how it works." Danae took a report out of her briefcase. "A Foundation consultant has developed a mathematical explanation which should please the skeptics."

Vince pointed to the report. "I want this to be in the trial record."

"I didn't have a chance to talk to Phil Bracken about the case before we flew up here. Would you give me the background?"

Danae said, "Let me fill you in. Steve Manteo lives in the Sierra Nevada Mountains north of Sacramento. Last winter, he was driving home when he came to a Rocky Butte Sheriff's Department search and rescue operation's command post. It was set up to search for a lost girl. He offered to help find the girl, and the Sheriff just blew him off. He sensed exactly where the girl was. The Sheriff refused to talk to him.

"Steve insisted in placing an 'X' locating the girl on the Sheriff's map on the wall. The Sheriff got mad and said the girl couldn't be in that area. He ordered Steve off the premises.

"Later that night, they found the girl frozen to death in the place marked on the map by Steve.

Vince placed both hands on the table and looked serious. "I read about the case and thought it would be an excellent opportunity to establish a legal precedent on the legitimacy of remote viewing. I had our corporate counsel file a civil suit on behalf of the parents of the girl against the Rocky Butte County Sheriff. The foundation is paying all the legal fees and expenses. All of any settlement will go to the girl's parents. Our counsel suggested we get Bracken & Stevens to handle the case. That is where you come in."

Danae nodded to Vince and said, "Here is the file. It's your case from here on out.

"Contact Candice Montgomery, in L.A., the consultant who wrote this report. She can get you up to speed on her theory. She is also writing a book to explain the theory of remote viewing to people with only eighth-grade mathematics training."

Danae made a note on her iPhone. "I'll call her, tell her you're working for us and ask her to contact you."

Vince stood. "You should go up to visit Steve, get to know him, and visit the area where the girl was lost. Danae, can you let Steve know Dave is coming? Danae will be your contact here at Colson." Vince shook my hand. "I'm delighted that you and Bracken & Stevens are handling this for us."

I feel like I am falling down a rabbit hole into a psychic wonderland.

Danae led the way out of the conference room to the lobby. She texted something on her iPhone and paused. "Your return transportation will be here in a few minutes. Are you comfortable with all this?"

"Yes, but I must say I've only started out on this learning curve."

If I didn't know that Colson has been a big client of Bracken & Stevens, I would recommend we walk away from this case.

Danae gestured with her finger as she spoke. "We wanted you to have a clean slate. But, I must warn you, the first time you discuss this subject with some scientists, you'll run into what I call 'The Bigot's Protocol.' They'll get incensed, maybe mad, turn red and lecture you on how any idea of psychic phenomena is pure gullibility. It's a hot button with many scientists and other people. Don't be discouraged: they're wrong, and we are right. But it's like telling a Southern tent-revival preacher there's no such thing as the Devil.

"Now, if you will excuse me, I've another meeting. A car will be here for you soon. I'm delighted you will be working this case."

I thought briefly about telling her of my vision but simply stated, "Thank you for selecting Bracken & Stevens to represent you."

In a few minutes, my town car arrived.

As I walked back into my office, Zaza said, "I thought you were going to Palo Alto."

"I did. These people are a fast company."

"Is there going to be an address in Palo Alto where I send flowers?" Zaza inquired sarcastically.

"No, this is going to be one-hundred percent business."

"Mr. Bracken asked for you to stop in when you got back. Shall I check to see whether he is available?"

"Yes."

Zaza had a brief telephone conversation with Patty, Bracken's secretary, then looked at me. "He's available."

Phil Bracken greeted me with a smile, stood up from his desk, and walked to his office leather couch. He motioned for me to sit in an adjacent chair. "Tell me about our new client."

"They move fast. They hold meetings that are three and a half minutes long and make important decisions in a snap."

Phil smiled. "Vince used to be a Navy jet pilot, the top-gun type. He is trained to assess things quickly, be decisive, and take action. If someone fires an anti-aircraft missile at you, you don't have time for a staff meeting; you simply begin evasive maneuvers. If you're coming in for a landing and all the red lights on the instrument panel flash and the flight controls stop working, you hit the eject button. It pays for a jet pilot to be decisive.

"If he hadn't liked you or failed to have an immediate confidence in you, he would have fired you on the spot. Congratulations on our new client."

If I survive this case with my reputation intact, I hope he will give me one of Colson's future cases.

"Danae seems to be as focused. I don't think she blinked her eyes all day. I doubt that I will be complaining about an indecisive client."

"Danae gave me the general outline of the case. What's your assessment?"

"I'll have to show that the Sheriff was negligent for not using all the search and rescue resources available, including the psychic.

Phil turned his head slightly. "The suit sounds rather straightforward."

"I'd like Elizabeth McKenzie to be my second chair in the trial. She has been valuable to me in other trials as a jury consultant."

"I'll arrange to have her assigned to you." Phil paused. "Do I sense you're uncomfortable with this."

"Frankly, I'm afraid I'll lose my scientific credibility among my peers in the patent law crowd. I might become the topic of jokes among my peers. Colson assures me that the scientific validity is there."

I hope so because it sounds crazy.

"Dave, we assigned you to this because if anyone can make a scientific argument, you can. Let me know if you start to think it isn't a solid case. We can pass the file off to one of the firms that specialize in legal circuses. Danae said Colson said he didn't want to go that way. He wants to establish the legal validity of this psychic stuff, as well as help the distressed parents.

"Keep me informed about developments." He rose from the couch, signaling the end of the meeting.

I was sweating, and my hands were wet. I was apprehensive about where this was taking my career.

As I returned to my office, Zaza asked, "Are you a bad boy? You look white."

"No, everything is fine,"

I don't think he is trying to get rid of me. What have I gotten myself into?

6

NEW AGE THINKING

I checked my email, then googled Remote Viewing. After reading a while, my thoughts turned to Raven. I texted her a message asking if she was free Friday night to teach me more about psychic phenomena.

Later, Raven called. "Can't do it Friday night. My friend Elise and I are going to a lecture about how people can learn to think effectively. Dr. Stahl, the speaker, is a psychic and best-selling author. A lot of West L.A. people consider him as their guru."

"That was what law school taught, thinking effectively." *I'd better be careful. My lawyer demeanor is coming out. That gets me in trouble with Raven.*

"Dr. Stahl's thinking is not the same as legal thinking. He teaches the value of intuition. It's what you might call a New Age way of thinking."

More of her New Age nonsense. I'll go because I want to see Raven again, and this will give us something to discuss later.

"Can I join you?"

"I'd like that. The meeting is Friday night at a hotel by the airport. I have a staff meeting after school, but I can meet you there. It starts at eight o'clock."

"Great. Want to make it dinner too?"

"I can't get there until after seven. I'll meet you in the lobby. Oh, by the way, it costs fifty bucks."

"No problem, My treat."

"In that case, it'll be one hundred bucks," she joked. "I have to go now. I'll see you in the main ballroom lobby of the Adventure Hotel just before seven-thirty on Friday. Bye."

"Bye."

She didn't seem friendly. I wish I could see her. I feel empty.

Friday at seven-thirty, I was in the lobby of the Adventure Hotel, one of the better places to stay at LAX. I peeked into the ballroom and was surprised that it sat hundreds of people. A few early birds sat near the front, hands in lap, eyes closed, smiling, meditating to New Age music. A door attendant told me to register and pointed to two women at a table. Those who were registering appeared normal. Professionals in business clothes, others in jeans, and casual attire. Many looked as if they bought their clothes at those trendy stores on Melrose Avenue where you can buy jeans with holes in the knees for a hundred-fifty dollars. I noticed two women with long brunette hair, combed straight, much longer than it might be natural. No doubt the product of an expensive Beverly Hills shop.

This isn't New Age. These people look like people you see everywhere in West L.A.

Raven approached, accompanied by another woman who had short black hair, in a pixie cut. She was in her early thirties and looked academic. They both looked as though they had come from a college classroom, in jeans, sneakers, and sweaters over simple tops.

The old wingman trick. Women appear with a friend when they need protection from unwanted advances or conversations.

Raven walked up and gave me a kiss on the cheek along with a firm hug, and backed away.

"Dave, this is Elise Benson."

"Hi Dave, Raven has told me all about you."

I felt naked. *I wonder what Raven said.*

"Elise did her Ph.D .dissertation in the study of psychic communication. If you want to know how it works, she's a good person to talk to. Her uncle is the one who predicts audience reactions to movies. Now, we had better register and stake out good seats."

I walked over and got in line to pay. Elise was behind me. When the registrar looked at me, I said "Three" and produced my credit card.

She ran my card and gave me three tickets and brochures of upcoming events. I handed one to Elise and one to Raven. Elise looked shocked.

"You didn't have to . . . ." stammered Elise.

"Yes, he did," interrupted Raven, smiling as she walked over, took my arm, and steered me to the entrance.

"All for research."

The ambiance of the room was electric, as the crowd is at a big football game waiting for the kickoff, or in a theater expecting the start of an acclaimed action movie. Old friends were greeting each other. Everyone was smiling and introducing themselves to people around them. I saw an actor I recognized–from a sitcom–but didn't know his name. We sat in a middle row of the ballroom, Raven next to me, Elise next to her.

I looked at the brochure. Tonight's topic was The Logic of Illogic.

I'm being sandbagged.

I read on. Tonight's session was a precursor to a two-day program, "New Ways To Think About Thought," which cost nine hundred dollars to attend.

These people are serious.

I had always assumed this New Age stuff was for hippies and bored housewives with nothing else to do but go to yoga classes and sit on the floor in cross-legged postures wearing designer exercise outfits. As I scanned the room, I calculated that the gross from this weekend event was something near a half-million dollars.

The lights lowered. The room quieted. Dr. Benjamin Stahl walked onto the stage smiling and greeting people in the audience. Everyone cheered and applauded. He sat on a comfortable chair in the middle of a small stage.

He picked up a microphone and smiled as he looked around the room. "It's a pleasure to be back in Los Angeles and see so many old friends. It's a pleasure to share this group energy, a bright spot in space-time. I welcome you all, to tonight's gathering and for those of you who stay the weekend, the weekend seminar. We've exciting things to share with you of what we call thought."

"But first, let us do a melding of our vibrations. Close your eyes and absorb the group energy."

Soft music came on as I closed my eyes. My mind and body relaxed. I felt very peaceful, and my thoughts of cautious judgment disappeared. After a few minutes, the music faded, and I heard Benjamin Stahl's voice again.

"You can open your eyes."

Raven squeezed my hand.

"The logic of illogic," he continued. "That is the sentence construction I love. One idea swallows another.

"Many in our western civilization think logic is the highest form of thought. It is only an overlay that our physical brain uses to interpret our surroundings. The physical universe existed long before our species evolved the part of our brains that allows what we call logical thinking. Medical journals report that people who have brain damage to certain areas cannot think logically

In the vastness of the space of the universe, in the plant and animal kingdoms, and the world within atoms, there is no such thing as logic."

I curled my finger into fists. *He never went to law school. Law and logic let us emerge from the dark ages. Logic is the basis of our sciences and technology. If it weren't for Raven, I'd walk out. This is nonsense.*

"The highest form of thinking is below or beyond your awareness. It is pre-symbolic, not logical. In this form of thinking, you are not thinking in words, numbers or pictures. Pre-symbolic thinking is conceptual, or emotional."

He lectured on and on describing the vagaries of our thought processes. After an hour, he looked at his watch and said, "Now, let's take a take a ten-minute break. When you come back, I will lead you through a meditation."

Everyone hurried from the room or talked to friends. I excused myself and went to the bathroom and then rejoined Raven and Elise in the ballroom lobby.

Raven had a big smile on her face. "What do you think about Dr. Stahl?"

"I'm almost overwhelmed. He's given me a lot to ponder." *I'll never understand why people need this metaphysical nonsense.*

"We should go back in now." Raven took my hand and led me back into the ballroom.

In a few minutes, Dr. Stahl took his seat on the stage and said, "Now, time for a meditation."

The lights dimmed, and Dr. Stahl led everyone through a guided meditation: Going to a meadow, sitting under a tree, exploring of the surroundings. I fell asleep after the first few minutes.

At the end of the session, as we were standing up ready to leave, Raven gave me a hug. "I'm glad you came. Thanks for the tickets" She turned toward Elise. The wingman thing was in play.

"Elise I would like to have lunch with you to discuss your research on psychic communication. It could be important for work I'm doing."

Raven smiled.

Elise handed me her business card "It must be tomorrow. I am leaving next week to give a paper in Chicago, and I am going from there to Cambridge. Call me in the morning."

I put the card in my pocket. "I can do that."

We exchanged hugs again. Raven's wasn't as stiff as when we met before the meeting.

I arrived early at Hernando's on Melrose hoping to get a good table. Hernando's is one of those trendy sidewalk restaurants with Mexican national colors in the awning and wrought iron tables and chairs separated from the sidewalk by only a thin iron railing. The place was filling with trendy West L.A. people wearing either business suits or designer jeans. Most of the women wore little makeup and had long slightly curled or straight hair.

Elise soon joined me, wearing jeans, but not the kind in the Melrose shops. She projected the image "I'm an academic.".

I rose and greeted her with a handshake which appeared proper. We exchanged small talk, ordered iced tea, and Hernando's famous tostadas.

"I understand that you are an attorney. Where does psychic communication fit into your practice?."

"I have a civil case involving a former psychic spy. Raven said your uncle who consults in Hollywood was an ex-psychic spy. I'd like to know what he does for clients."

"He did work for the CIA, but he doesn't talk about it much. Until only a few years ago when the CIA declassified the program we thought he worked for a money management company. He said he couldn't talk about his work because of client's confidentiality agreements. When I was exploring subjects for my Ph.D. dissertation, he agreed to explain how he did his remote viewing."

"I will soon be standing in front of a jury making that same explanation. I read a book describing remote viewing written by another former CIA psychic spy. It said little nothing of how it works. Does your dissertation go into that?"

"It covers the broad subject of clairvoyance, including remote viewing. It's case studies of documented and verified happenings. I focused on proving that it happens. I'll send you a copy. It would take too long to explain."

"Can you give me a summary?"

She adjusted the silverware in front of her. "Certainly. First, clairvoyance is real and fairly common. People often don't know when it is happening. It's real, and it's pre-symbolic."

I adjusted my silverware. "That's quite a jump of belief. Let me parse your sentence. What is clairvoyance?"

"Dr. Stahl said in his lecture last night that basic thought is in our subconscious at a pre-symbolic level, including mental pictures. For instance, I can mentally picture my cat, Billy, and recall the emotions I have about him. That is the pre-symbolic level. If I want to send you a text message describing him, I have to convert the idea of Billy to words or symbols. When you read my text message, you may change the word 'cat' to your picture of a cat. If you had visited my house and knew Billy, you could make a picture in your mind of Billy.

"If something happened to Billy just before I came here, I might have a lot of attention on him. You, not knowing me, might sense my attention was somewhere else. In the course of our conversation, you might bring up the subject of cats.

"If we were close friends, and you had been over to my house and played with Billy, sometime in our conversation you might ask, 'How is Billy?'

"The abstract idea of cats or Billy would be psychically communicated."

I thought for a while. "I guess I've had that experience. But, that is anecdotal."

She sat upright and seemed more authoritative. "In my work, I started by assuming that clairvoyance exists. I've been exploring what conditions cause and limit it."

"In my lawsuit, a psychic spy came across a search and rescue operation near where he lives in the Sierra Nevada Mountain Range. He inquired and saw a picture of a lost girl He returned to his car. As he sat, he suddenly knew where the girl was and had a general feeling of how the girl felt and what she saw."

Elise relaxed from her authoritative posture. "That's the kind of clairvoyance I studied."

"I will visit him soon so I can hear his story firsthand."

"What is the difference between clairvoyance and remote viewing?"

"They're the same. Both sense something in another time and space. My uncle said they used the term 'clairvoyance' at the start of the intelligence program but change it to 'remote viewing' so that the military didn't associate the program with storefront fortune tellers, mystics, or the other kinds of people involved in psychic activities. The term 'remote viewing' pertained to what they were doing in the intelligence program. Changing the name got rid of a lot of baggage other words carried."

I was still confused. "The remote viewer that is the subject of my lawsuit is called a psychic spy in his book. Why don't they call him a clairvoyant?"

She smiled. "The publisher added that name to widen his audience."

"Good! I'm glad you cleared that up. In my trial arguments, I'll be careful to define 'remote viewing' and not let it get confused other psychic activities or practices."

"I'm sure exposure to the facts of the case will convince you." Elise was interrupted by the waitress serving our tostadas.

Elise started to eat. "The ability of the remote viewer to know where the lost girl was and how she felt are excellent examples of what Dr. Stahl called pre-symbolic communication. The message he received was not in the form of words."

We engaged in small talk while we ate. As we were finishing, Elise gave me a stern look. "Raven is one of my dearest friends. How long have you been seeing her?"

"Three months. We haven't been dating all that time because my travel for work created gaps in our being together."

"You should be very careful with her. She's very vulnerable."

"Vulnerable? I don't understand. Is she weak? Do people take advantage of her?"

"I should have said emotionally vulnerable. For women, that means being willing or able to put ourselves out there emotionally and go into the depths of feeling. It's like playing Texas Hold'em poker and being able to go all-in. We're willing to bet all our chips, except they are emotional chips."

She saw the confused expression on my face. "Perhaps you should attend next time Dr. Stahl conducts a workshop on vulnerability."

"I'll ask Raven to tell me when that workshop is scheduled."

7

CANDICE

Back in my office I found I'd received a text message from Danae saying she had contacted Candice Montgomery who would give me a call

Mid-afternoon, Zaza buzzed me. "There is a Candice Montgomery calling. I don't know which one she is."

I picked up the phone and said, "Hello, this is David Willard."

"Mr. Willard, I'm Candice Montgomery, a consultant for the Colson Foundation. Danae Hamilton asked me to call."

"Pleased to meet you. I'm also working for them. They have me trying a civil case involving remote viewing. Are you familiar with that?"

"Yes, I collaborated on a paper with one of the former members of the CIA remote viewing program two years ago. That paper resulted in me being called on by the Colson Foundation to do more work. We've a good working relationship."

She sounded formal, defensive, so I explained, "They were in awe of your work. I've spent most of my career as a patent attorney working in high-tech. The only thing I know of remote viewing is what I read in a book by Steve Manteo. Colson said he wanted me on the case because I'm starting with a clean slate on the subject. They said I should talk to you. I'll be your student. I may want to use you as an expert witness in the civil case."

"That's good to know. But, I can't do a good job talking about my research on the phone without a blackboard or visual aids. I've other business in your area first thing tomorrow morning. Can I meet you at your office about ten?"

"That's fine with me. Let's make it lunch too."

She agreed.

"You might read my introductory book on eight-dimensional theory. You can download it from my website. I'll email you a link."

I hung up the telephone. *What have I gotten myself into?* The email arrived, and I downloaded her book. *The teacher is assigning me homework.*

I spent the early morning reading her book. It described the CIA's remote viewing program. I looked at the references. She had been writing papers on eight-dimensional space theory for over a decade.

This is great. At last, I am getting rational thought.

I refreshed my memory on mathematical concepts with Wikipedia. I googled Candice and found she was born in Louisiana and lived on a Native American reservation. It didn't show her personal history, but it said she earned her Ph.D. in math from Tulane University.

At ten o'clock, Zaza buzzed me and said, "Your visitor is in the conference room."

Candice was of average height with a frail build. She was wearing a long, black, pleated dress, matching her long straight black hair. Her bronze complexion suggested her mixed racial heritage.

"Candice, how nice to meet you in person."

Her wide, brown eyes portrayed a mix of great curiosity and admiration. When Candice looked at me, it was as though I was the most amazing person she'd ever met. She got right to the point. "Tell me about your science and math background to give me a frame of reference. Also, tell me about the case you're working on."

I described my undergraduate scientific education and described my more technical patent cases. Then I summarized the Colson case and mentioned that the trial would be in the court in Rocky Butte.

"It sounds like another Scopes Trial," she observed.

"I'm surprised you know of that trial. We lawyers call it The State of Tennessee vs. Scopes."

Candice laughed. "I'm not a legal scholar. My husband, Tom, and I are old movie buffs. We rented and watched the 1960 *Inherit The Wind.*

"I remember the movie well. It was a trial of a teacher who was teaching evolution in a state that had laws dictating that only Creationism should be taught. Underneath, it was about people's reaction to ideas contrary to their firmly held beliefs.

"I see the same thing at mathematics conventions. Somebody will present a paper with a new idea in mathematics and many wise old men will attack them to defend old beliefs on the subject."

"This sounds like a touchy subject."

"Yes, I've been burnt or should I say roasted, after presenting new ideas at conferences."

"If you agree to be an expert witness at the trial, I promise I won't let anybody attack you in court.

"The descriptions of the Rocky Butte Sheriff I read in the case files make him sound like a redneck. I'll be challenging his, and the jury's, conventional scientific belief system they learned in high school."

Candice said, "I love this. It appeals to the iconoclast in me. Go on."

"Instead of a contest between the Biblical beliefs and science, as in the Scopes trial, I must overcome the old science beliefs and show them how new ideas in science are possible. I guess that's where you come in."

Candice smiled. "That's where the Colson Foundation comes in. They hired me to write the book I posted on my website."

I nodded. in agreement. "I used the link you sent me to download a copy and have been studying it. It is well done."

"I'm glad you liked it. What you know of higher-dimensional realities?"

"Only what I have assimilated from the first chapters of your book. I don't understand how this fits with what I have heard about ascended spirits and other planes and dimensions of existence."

Candice laughed. "Oh! I'm not talking about metaphysical stuff. That's another set of beliefs. I'm talking mathematics and physics."

I gave her a blank stare.

Candice looked around the conference room and walked over to a tray of muffins. She took a large muffin, placed it on a paper plate, picked up a plastic fork and knife, returned to the table. "I'm not going to eat this."

No kidding. She doesn't look like somebody who eats many muffins. I continued my blank stare.

She pointed to the muffin with her knife and said, "Suppose the whole muffin is the totality of physical laws. She cut the muffin in half and said, "This half represents four-dimensional physics and science–the kind you learned in school. That is based on the idea of four-dimensions, up-down, right-left, backwards-forwards, and time. Four-dimensional physics explain the everyday physical experience."

I looked at the muffin. *That looks good. Maybe it's time for a snack.*

"Many people develop a dogmatic faith in their four-dimensional science. They believe it can explain everything. If something doesn't fit their scientific ideas, they ignore, attack, or dismiss it."

"Excuse me; my attention is stuck on that muffin. Are we going to split it between us?"

She laughed. "In a minute, if you like."

"I have to admit that before I read your book. I believed conventional science explained everything, except for the things that exist in the strange world down the rabbit hole of quantum mechanics."

Are we going talk science or eat that muffin?

She probed the muffin with her knife. "Scientists have another little secret. In astrophysics, the equations of four-dimensional science say the universe should be collapsing like a balloon leaking air. Instead, the data from observatories with big telescopes shows the universe is expanding. Something is blowing up the balloon! To explain this discrepancy, scientists had to invent 'dark energy and dark matter' and say it represents Ninety-five percent of the universe; they don't even know how or where to find it."

"Ninety-five percent. That's a hell of a fudge factor. What is wrong with saying God is blowing the universe up like a big balloon? That is easier for me to believe in than elusive dark matter." My stomach grumbled. *When are we going to deal with the muffin?*

Candice pointed to the other half of the muffin. "Science is a missing a piece in the puzzle, a simple one. If one says the four dimensions, up-down, right-left, backwards-forwards, and time, are complex numbers the universe can be described as eight-dimensional."

She moved the two halves of the muffin together. "Now we have a complete science. The equations of eight-dimensional physics predict many of things four-dimensional science says can't exist. With eight-dimensional physics, you don't need dark matter to explain how the universe is behaving. But that is another topic."

"I'll save that for later, until after I understand the eight-dimensional thing."

She noticed I was staring at the muffin. "I will fix myself some tea. Take the muffin. You can have all eight dimensions of it."

We had a break. I ate the muffin.

"Okay, but what does your mathematical research mean for my lawsuit?"

"It means that science can explain how your psychic spy could have known the location of the lost girl."

"If he had had a muffin?"

I must figure out how to explain this to a jury of rural Rocky Butte people. A dozen muffins. I doubt Judge Cartwright will allow that.

"No, it is not about muffins. In eight dimensions, information is transferred between physical brains by means other than the usual radio waves, lasers, or wires."

I felt confused "You had better start with at the beginning to explain this."

Candice leaned forward as though she was sharing a confidence with me. "In classical physics There is something called Maxwell's Equations that are used to explain all electromagnetic things. In 1861 Maxwell came up with twenty equations that described the behavior of all electromagnetic phenomenon; electricity, light etc. Two decades later physicists Heaviside and Hertz reduced Maxwell's (four dimensional) twenty equations into four. These four are today's official Maxwell's Equations referred to by engineers and physicists.

Skeptics of the existence ESP or clairvoyance say that Maxwell's Equations prove that mind-to-mind communication is impossible."

"Yes, Candice, I have had that lecture from a scientist that consults with me on patents. So where is the loophole?"

"When they reduced the twenty equations to four they 'threw out a baby' with the bathwater." I went back to Maxwell's original twenty equations, rewrote them in terms of eight-dimensions, and found that they work for ESP and clairvoyance!"

I shook my head and acted like I was trying to shake water out of my ear. "That's great to hear. But, my cup runneth over. I can't get my mind around this right now. Let's go have lunch and talk about something else for a while."

Captain Ahab's is one of those theme restaurants from twenty years ago, with antique diving helmets, worn ropes, fishing nets, and oars decorating the walls. Our table was a recycled boat hatch covered a variety of seashells sealed in epoxy. The informality of the restaurant is a welcome break from our stern office surroundings and a good place to talk and develop rapport.

We chatted as we read the menu and ordered. Candice declined my suggestion of wine.

"Only on special occasions, and, besides, I'm working today." She rolled her big brown eyes.

"I guess I should abstain if I will try to keep up with you this afternoon. Tell me what you do when you're not a mathematician or a teacher."

"We live on the edge of the mountains of the Angeles National Forest in Altadena. I love just being there, enjoying our lovely home, and watching the wildlife from our backyard. We hike in the mountains behind us and go to the Sierras when we've time."

"We?'

"My significant other, Tom Watson, is a Hollywood composer who arranges music for movies and television. He works on scores at home most of the time. He also counsels people, helps them with their problems. We meditate together and have many close friends who are spiritually oriented. We've lots of flexible time to enjoy being with each other. She paused. "So, what do you do when you're not an attorney?"

"I spend time in the desert in a place called CrystalSky. It's over the mountains, north of where you live in Altadena. I have a sailplane and a cottage near the airport. I often soar for hours a day. From my porch, on a clear day, I can see a hundred miles to the southern Sierras. I've learned to enjoy the desert, the open space, the flora, and fauna."

There was a pause. I felt she was waiting for the "we" part.

She looked away. "My grandfather was a Native American. When I was little, we lived with him in Oklahoma for a few weeks each summer. We used to hike together, and sometimes we sat and watched the soaring birds. He said you could learn much from them.

"Enough about me. It sounds the soaring thing is important to you. Do you take people for rides? Any pilots in your family?"

"No. My father had a hardware store in a small northern California logging town. My mother was a schoolteacher. They raised me with Midwestern Baptist values. Not a single shaman in the family.

"Five years ago someone gave me a Christmas gift of a certificate for a glider ride. I tried it once and was hooked. Soaring is esthetic experience, It's very like boat sailing, except more is happening.

"Sometimes, I can't make it back to the airport and have to be retrieved by a tow plane or a ground crew. There are survival hazards in landing in the middle of nowhere in the desert when it is a hundred degrees."

Candice's eyes grew wide with interest or amazement as I talked. "You're passionate about this soaring thing! I wouldn't want to end the day in the middle of nowhere. Soaring must be fun to risk that."

I shook my head. "If I'm very scientific in my decisions during a flight, I end up at my home airport."

Lunch came. We chatted only of the meal and food for a while.

"If you write a mathematical paper, don't you have to risk going through a peer review editing process? I'd rather end up landing in the desert than risk being torn apart by a bunch of know-it-all professors."

"At a state college the emphasis is more on teaching, and they let me publish without review. "If people disagree with me, that's their problem. If the work is useful, people will build on the ideas. If the work is of no value, it is forgotten."

She sat up straight with some apparent pride. "I've been doing papers on the implications of complex eight-dimensional space theory for more than a decade. I ignore the academic critics with conflicting pet theories to defend."

I nodded my head in agreement. "What do you do with your students who balk at accepting eight-space?"

"Some students scoff and object to my broaching the subject of clairvoyance in discussions of eight-space. I tell them they can believe it or not as they wish, but eight-space questions will be on the final exam."

I thought for a minute. "I'll have to convince a jury without being able to threaten them with a bad grade.

Back at my office, we returned to the conference room, and Candice described her book.

"The Foundation had me in write a book, A Friendly Guide to the Theory of Clairvoyance." It's for anyone with high school mathematics."

"Is that the one I downloaded from your site yesterday?

"Yes. With a different title."

Candice described the book. She looked concerned. "What do you think?"

"We'll have you summarize the book and enter it as evidence. You testify that the theory presented is valid. Your candid attitude will work in convincing a jury. I'll get another expert witness to validate your testimony."

"That should work. We've covered many subjects. Is this enough for one day?"

"Yes. You gave me a strategy for presenting the subject to the jury. Thank you so much for coming by for this lesson. Is any of this going to be on the test?"

She laughed. "You can be sure."

I walked Candice out of the conference room to the lobby. "This has been enlightening."

"I enjoyed taking to you." She dug into her purse for a second. "Here is Tom's card. You might like to spend time him. He counsels people in how to mentally travel in space-time.

"Thanks," She left. *Mentally travel in space-time?*

Carolyn gave me her 'I'm fascinating and available!' smile.

After five minutes in my office, Zaza buzzed me. "Carolyn says your cutie is back in the lobby and wants to talk with you."

I hurried to the lobby and saw Candice with her eyes opened even wider than before. "Someone was hanging around my car when I got to the garage. Could you check it out for me? He was up to something. He ran down the parking ramp instead of back into the lobby when he saw me."

I gestured to Carolyn. "Please call Mr. Steel in building security. Tell him to meet us in the visitor's parking area."

Carolyn gave me her "Oh, this is so important, and I want to please you smile."

I turned to Candice. "Did you get a good look at him?"

"No. He was too far away. I can tell you he was a male Caucasian, about five-five, stocky build, gray crew cut, round gold-rimmed glasses, wearing khaki pants, and a white business shirt, no tie."

"Good description! Danae asked me to report anything suspicious to her. I'll get security to make a report, and will forward it."

We took the elevator to the building lobby and started toward the door to the garage. Then, I heard, "Mr. Willard, is there a problem?" I introduced Steel to Candice, and she related her encounter.

"The surveillance camera in that area isn't working today. Let's go look at your car." As we entered the garage, Steel looked around. "Where did you see him?"

"I was right there by the driver's side of the car."

"Which car is yours?" Steel asked.

"That blue Volvo over there."

That's not the most likely model for a car thief to choose in this building full of high-priced lawyers.

We stood back as Steel checked under the hood, examined the interior, and shined a flashlight underneath the body. In a few minutes, he came and reported. "Two unusual things: There is a symbol drawn in the dust on the windshield and somebody wiped the dirt from the door, as though they were eliminating fingerprints. Otherwise, it looks as if everything is normal."

Steel took notes of everything Candice had said. He used his iPhone to photograph the symbol on the windshield. It looked like a Mayan hieroglyph, a square with a stocky stick figure in it.

Steel took his last photo. "Do you have any idea what this mark is or what it may mean?"

We both shook our heads to say no. Steel offered to test-drive the car, and Candice agreed. He drove the car down to the next garage level.

I looked at Candice. She looks frightened. I'd better make sure she is okay to drive.

We could hear the tires squealing and his gunning the engine and braking. Steel returned. "It seems perfect. Just to be safe, have someone in a garage put it on a hoist. I can't see much without crawling under."

Candice nodded in agreement. "It's due for a lube service. I'll have it done tomorrow."

I turned to Steel. "Please give me a full written report. We're working on an unusual court case, and it might have something to do with it."

Steel nodded yes. "Give me your keys, and I'll check your car out."

"Candice, let's go back into the conference room and have a cup of tea while you burn off that adrenaline."

"Good idea. I'm shaky."

We chatted for fifteen minutes as I asked her to tell me more about her summers with her grandfather in Oklahoma. Then she smiled. "I'm okay now."

"I'll walk you to your car."

As Candice and I walked through the lobby on the way to the elevator, Carolyn gave me her 'you're so wonderful' smile.'

Within a few minutes of being back at my desk, Steel appeared. He was carrying a little black box in a plastic sack. "I found this on your car concealed under a fender. It's a GPS tracking device. Is it yours or part of an anti-theft system?"

"Neither." *What the hell?.*

"This is a law enforcement model. It's not the cheap consumer quality. Any idea who planted this or why?"

"I have no idea."

"Do you want me to scan your car every day for a while?"

"Good idea." I returned to my office and sent a brief email to Danae describing what had happened. In thirty seconds, she replied instructing me to send a report to a firm she identified as their security consultants, EB Services.

Somebody bugging my car and maybe stalking me! I became incensed. *I need to talk to the building administrator. We need more security in the garage. We pay hight rent for offices in this building. We shouldn't have people tampering with our cars.*

8

THE WAVE

I spent the rest of the week preparing my case–reading about remote viewing, and delving into the mathematics that Candice used to explain how clairvoyance works. Friday morning, I received an email from a friend at the Aviation Weather Station at LAX, who is also a soaring pilot. A late season cold front was approaching. Tomorrow, about noon, a mountain wave could form over CrystalSky.

I got excited. As the cold front approaches, the wind over the mountains forms a wave that can be tens of thousands of feet high. Sailplanes can "surf" along a mountain wave They're fun.

I thought for a minute. Raven might be on lunch break. I called Raven on her cell. "Hi, stranger. "What's up?" "How's school going?"

"Great! I had the final exam in my night school class last night. This course was a tough one, statistics. It's required for my Masters. Math isn't my thing. How's your new court case?

My friend Elise told me it was about clairvoyance. I'm not sure what that is.?"

"It's getting very interesting and puzzling. Do you remember how disturbed I was after I had that vision while waiting to be retrieved from the dry lake?"

"How could I forget? You were really shaken up."

"Do you remember me talking about my associate Rodger? Well, when I got back to L.A. I found out that he died in a freeway accident at about the same time I had the vision. My vision was accurate!"

"That's amazing!" She paused for a minute."That's heavy. How do you feel about that?"

"Okay. A year ago, I would have let myself forget about it or rationalize that it didn't happen. The scientist in me used to say such things were impossible. I had my vision and sensed what Rodger experienced in the accident. I have to admit it was clairvoyant and real."

"What a coincidence! What is the scientist in you feeling now?"

"Before now, the scientist got upset whenever someone talked about psychic stuff."

"Oh really? I guess I have to agree."

"Now, I can't ignore my vision experience. I can approach the subject with an open mind."

"I'd love to talk about this more. It's not a good time now. I have to get back to class. Fridays are always hectic."

"I'm going to the desert tomorrow, just for the day. Be back late afternoon or evening. Would you like to come along and we could talk more about this? I'll even take you for what might be a spectacular glider ride."

"You've called at a good time. I need a day off from grading papers and cramming for exams. You know how I love the desert. I do have to get back tomorrow evening. About the glider ride: we've been intimate before, but won't both of us in that little cockpit on your sailplane be a little too friendly? You barely fit in alone."

"I'll rent a glider from the flying school. They have two big seats, one behind the other for instructors and students."

"Don't you have to prepare for your court case?"

"I think I need a day off for my mind to assimilate all the new ideas. Tomorrow is an unusual weather day, one that might happen only every year or two, producing a wave at CrystalSky. Flying on wave days is fun."

"I don't understand. There is no lake or other water at CrystalSky. How can there be waves?"

"The waves are in the wind blowing over the mountains. I'll tell you about it on the drive out there."

"Okay. I'll go with you if you can assure me there are two seats. Can I bring a picnic lunch?"

"Wonderful! It'll be cold so bring a jacket." After we had made meeting arrangements, I hung up the phone. *I like this lady, I wonder where she buys her perky pills.* I noticed I felt a nice warm feeling in my heart region.

When I was a few minutes away from Raven's apartment, I called. "I'm only a few blocks away."

"I'll meet you in front of my apartment so you won't have to park."

Again, I noticed this unusual feeling or energy around my heart. *Interesting.* As I turned the corner onto her street, I saw her standing at the curb, wearing light blue jeans, white tennis shoes, and a brown patterned blouse.

A nice leggy look.

She saw me, grinned, picked up her picnic basket and down jacket, and stepped off the curb. As I stopped, she put the basket and her jacket in the back seat of the car, slid over, and gave me a kiss on the cheek.

She looked at me in mock seriousness."Two seats in the glider–you promised?" That broke the ice, and I laughed.

"I called the airport and they've reserved a two-seater for us."

"Are we going to fly far or land somewhere else? Should I bring the picnic in case we get stranded on that dry lake?"

"No. We'll take off and get towed toward the mountains. If we're lucky, there'll be a wave we can fly back and forth on. We might fly for about an hour and land back where we started."

"What is a wave doing in the desert?"

"The wind blows north from L.A. into the desert before a storm. If it's at the right speed and headed in the right direction, the wind does a thing like water flowing over a rock in a creek rapids. It flows down and then jumps up into a wave.

This desert wave can go up tens of thousands of feet. You're in for a great experience."

Raven smiled her impish smile. "This sounds like fun or maybe a little scary?"

"Definitely fun."

After a long pause, Raven looked at me with concern. "Do you want to tell me how the vision you had on our last outing was related to something that really happened."

I retold her the story.

'That's terrible! That must have been a real shock. You seem okay with it now."

"After reflecting on it for a while and learning about clairvoyance and remote viewing, the lawyer in me has decided I can be open minded."

We exited the freeway to get gas. After our stop, when Raven got back in the car carrying two cups of coffee, she had her impish grin. She was up to something.

"It's cold and the clouds look like rain. Are we really going soaring or is this some kind of trick?"

I laughed and said, "No, this is good wave weather."

"I'd better see this wave or else I'll never believe anything you say again. This trip had better not be a version of 'come up to my place, and I'll show you my etchings.' Here, I have a treat for you."

She reached into her jacket pocket and produced two Snickers bars. She unwrapped the end of one and handed it to me. "Try this,"

"Oh, no thanks, I'm not much on sweets."

"How long has it been since you've eaten one of these?"

"I can't remember the last time."

"A few minuted ago I heard the lawyer say he is trying to be more open minded. Try being open minded about this Snickers bar! Trust me, they're good. There's little to lose in eating a candy bar. Go for it!"

I took a bite and said, "This is okay."

She unwrapped her bar, took a bite, and an expression of great pleasure came over her face.

"Sometimes, I'd do anything for a Snickers bar."

"I'll bear that in mind."

She laughed, unbuckled her seatbelt and slid over next to me and said, "Are we almost there, yet?"

After about a minute of silence, while she snuggled, she said, "I know a fun game to pass the time. You concentrate on a picture of something, and I'll try to tell you what it is. See if I can make an ESP connection between us."

She paused and seemed to feel that I continued to be uncomfortable with the psychic stuff.

"Trust me. Give it a try. Start now." She closed her eyes.

I stared down the road.

After about twenty seconds she opened her eyes and turned to me, "It looks like something red, a red spot, and it's bouncing up and down, kind of like a yo-yo. What were you picturing?"

She saw the shocked expression on my face. "Come on, don't cheat, tell me."

"I was watching the red taillight on the car in front of us. It's moving up and down because the road is uneven. That's amazing! Can you read my mind?"

"No, that's a kind of game my brother and I invented as kids for when we were on trips with my parents. All I can get is vague images. I sense some of your feelings when we talk. For instance, right now you're a little upset, not with me, but with the idea I can know what you're seeing."

"You're right. I understand about ESP on an intellectual level, but it's against my scientific training. How do you change an ingrained belief system?"

"Exposure and discussion are what I use. Some of the high school students I teach have weird belief systems. The first step seems to be getting them off their cushion of certainty in what they are certain of."

We were silent for a while as Raven looked at the scenery. The trip from L.A. to the desert starts with industrial buildings lining the freeway. That scene gives way to older housing tracts with an abundance of trees. Then, as one moves to the desert, the newer housing tracts have fewer trees. After that, the countryside turns to dry chaparral-covered hills and occasional mobile homes. In places, isolated tracts of homes are crowded together a few feet apart, surrounded by high beige cinder block walls. They sit like islands in the desert.

"I don't know much about you," said Raven. "Where were you born, raised, and what was it like where you grew up? Who were your friends?"

We told each other stories until we reached our turn onto the road leading to CrystalSky Airport. Raven looked at the gray sky. "It's overcast, you can't even see the tops of the mountains. It doesn't look like a soaring day."

"This is the kind of day a wave develops. If the wind shifts a little bit, it'll be just right for a wave. We'd better be ready to fly when the condition appears."

We drove to the operations building, a weather-worn mobile home with a swamp cooler on top. The door was open, and inside I met Dan the tow pilot. Raven stayed outside and looked at the sky and mountains. I rented the high-performance two-place sailplane. Dan told the office girl, Celia, to tow it to the take-off line with the ATV.

Dan looked concerned. "The other day there was a strange, nerdy guy out here who asked which sailplane trailer belonged to you. He looked it over for a while but didn't get into it or do anything, as far as I could tell."

"Thanks, I'll check it out after we're ready to fly. I don't want to miss the wave." I paused. "Was he a white, male Caucasian, five-five, stocky build, gray crew cut, wearing gold-rimmed glasses?"

Dan looked puzzled. "Yes, a friend of yours?"

"No, but please call me at home or work if you ever see him again."

I glanced at the vending machine at the end office. "Is that thing working?"

"Yes. We don't turn it off 'till the weather gets hot."

I put two dollar bills on the counter. "Will you give me eight quarters."

Outside, I joined Raven as she looked at the two-place sailplane. "Wow, the wings are big and shiny, and they have these cute little ears going up at the ends."

"The wingspread is eighteen meters, about sixty feet. This one is a lot harder to put together than mine, which is only fifteen meters. These things at the end make it fly farther."

"Are you sure we can make it back to the airport?"

"Absolutely! We will never be more than ten miles from here."

"Do I get to sit in front or back?"

"Front. I can fly from the back seat and see over your shoulders."

I completed my preflight check, inspecting the wings, tail, controls, and cockpit.

Everything looks all right. Celia came with the ATV, and I hooked the rope to the big sailplane.

"Raven, the sailplane only has one wheel under the pilot's seat. We need to walk and hold up the wing tips, so they don't drag on the ground."

Celia towed us to the staging area.

"Let's see how you fit in the front seat."

Raven got in, and I showed her how to adjust the seatbelt and shoulder harness.

Raven joked, "Maybe I should have worn a sports bra. These shoulder straps don't do much for a girl's figure. They are more flattering if I spread them outside my boobies like this."

How can I keep my mind on flying?

"You might not like the way they're squeezed by the straps we hit a downdraft. I won't be looking at your figure. I'll be behind you, and busy."

Intriguing idea: watching them bounce up and down.

"Are you warm enough?"

"Yes."

We sat down in the dirt next to the sailplane, leaned our backs against the hull. We opened our thermos of coffee and warmed our hands on the cups as we drank.

Raven stared at the sky. "I don't see a wave. What does it look like?"

"We can't see it. We have to look for signs it is there." I picked up a small rock and drew a triangle in the dirt. "Here is the crest of the mountain. The wind and clouds are streaming in a straight line. When wind direction and speed are just right, the wind and clouds stream down the side like this." I drew the line for the wind going down the side of the triangle. "The clouds evaporate as the wind goes lower, a gap in the clouds forms. It looks as though someone unzips the clouds along the mountains and reveals the clear blue sky.

"The invisible wind keeps going down. Then, it turns around and goes up." I drew the line going up much higher than the crest. "We fly our sailplanes on that up-going air like

"Where does the wind go? It can't go up forever." Raven pointed to my dirt-diagram.

"It eventually turns around and comes down and forms the back side of the wave. Today, the back of the wave might only be a half-mile downwind from the front." I drew the wind going up and then turning around and falling.

Raven looked at the diagram and then looked at me. "How do you know all this?"

"NASA has studied waves. Weather forecasters now predict when and where they might occur. Over the Rockies or Sierras, the waves can be fifty-thousand or more feet high. When airlines fly into the down part of big waves, passengers can fly out of their seats. Air traffic controllers route airliners away from waves."

Raven nodded. "I was on a flight from Chicago to San Francisco one time when that happened. We all thought we were going to die. People were screaming. One man got a bloody gash in his head. Now, I always wear my seatbelt on airlines."

"It's will be a little like that for a while today. When the front of the wave is only a half-mile from the back, the air gets churned up in-between." I scratched swirly lines in my dirt-diagram between the front and back part of the wave. "There are huge bubbles of air going up next to bubbles of air going down. We call that area the rotor."

"Can you see the bubbles?"

"You will know it when you are in one kind or the other. Our shoulder harnesses and seat-belts will hold us from rattling around. We will have to fly through the bottom part of the rotor for a while to get to the smooth wave. On some days a cloud forms and rolls around in the rotor."

"It all sounds scary."

"We will have a turbulent ride for only a few minutes. There are thrilling aesthetic experiences to be had flying among and above the clouds. Today could be one of those days."

I looked at Raven. "Somehow, I wanted to share this with you."

That's true, but I didn't expect to say it.

Raven looked back at me with soft eyes "I'm glad."

Dan walked over and said, "Look, the gap is forming in the eastern part of the ridge. Better get ready to go in a few minutes." He walked to the tow plane and climbed in.

We got up and brushed the dust off our pants. We rolled the big plane to the center of the runway. I helped Raven strap herself in and got into the back seat. "I'll go through my check sheet, and then we'll be ready to go. We'll wait until the wave gets more established."

The clouds were streaming over the mountains, and the whole sky was overcast. As the wind shifted direction, the gap widened on our side of the mountain.

Raven tugged at the shoulder harness and wiggled in the seat. "Amazing. It's as though someone is unzipping the clouds along the mountains to show us the clear blue sky."

Celia came over to assist in our takeoff. The Pawnee's engine coughed, belched blue smoke and then hummed. Celia attached the Pawnee's two-hundred foot tow rope to the sailplane and then picked up the wingtip. She gave me a thumbs-up.

My adrenaline rose. *I never get used to this part.*

"Raven, Ready to go?"

"Yes, this is scary!"

The rudder pedals thumped as I wiggled the tail to signal Dan.

The Pawnee engine roared at full throttle.

"Here we go!"

We rumbled down the rough gravel runway and in a few seconds we were airborne. I held it few inches above the ground until the tow plane got to full speed.

Raven laughed. "Whee, this is fun! I'm flying."

The tow plane rocked back and climbed. I pulled back on the stick and followed.

"In a few minutes, it'll get turbulent. The tow plane will climb a hundred feet or fall a hundred feet, we will fly through the bottom of the rotor and I will follow. It'll be like a roller coaster ride, but won't last long."

There was quiet for a few minutes as Raven looked down. "This is fun! Look, there's the Devil's Punchbowl. It looks so different from up here."

Bump! The sailplane groaned.

"What was that?" Raven grabbed a handle on the side of the cockpit.

"The turbulence I told you about."

"Is this okay?"

"Yes" You haven't felt anything yet.

The tow plane shot up to forty-five degrees above us at the other end of the two hundred foot tow rope.

Raven held on tighter. "Why is he doing that?"

I pulled hard back on the stick to follow. A second later we were pushed down in our seats as the sailplane hit the same updraft. We chased the tow plane up. It then almost disappeared below us in a downdraft. We were thrust upward against our shoulder harnesses until our heads nearly bumped the canopy. Then, the tow plane was above us again, and we sank down in our seats.

Raven groaned. "You said this would to be fun. I feel like I weigh two-hundred pounds."

I looked at the G-meter acceleration gauge. Two G's. "Right now you do."

I had a brief thought. *Bouncing up and down, up and down. I wonder if Victoria's Secret can take it.*

After a few minutes of this roller coaster ride, the sailplane groaned as we were thrust down in our seats, Raven asked in grunt, "Are we almost there, yet? Is this your idea of a good time? You promised fun."

I knew she was kidding. "We are almost through the rotor."

In a few seconds, the turbulence vanished. Astounding silence. The tow plane stopped moving up and down and seemed to hover. Twang! The tow plane dove away.

"What was that? Did something break."

"I released the tow rope. Everything is okay."

Raven let go of her tight grip on the handle on the side of the cockpit.

We were several thousand feet below the mountain peaks and the gap in the clouds.

"I'll fly toward the mountains and get into the stronger part of the wave. Do you see that gauge on the left-hand side of the instrument panel?"

"The one pointing to the number one?"

'That says we are climbing at one-hundred feet per minute. Watch as I get closer to the mountain."

Raven grabbed onto the handle again. "We are flying straight into the side of the mountain! That's where you said the air was going down. Shouldn't we turn away!"

"It's okay. Watch the mountain."

Raven swallowed. "It's falling away like it is painted on a window shade that someone is pulling down."

"See, the gauge is reading eight hundred feet per minute.

I turned to fly along the cloud gap. The air was as smooth as glass, and the sailplane flew in silence, buoyed by an invisible force.

We floated up through the gap. Now higher than the mountains, we could see the flat sea of low clouds to the south, covering LA, stretching hundreds of miles.

Raven let go of the handle. "I'm starting to relax. This part is fun. It's so quiet and graceful. This is like the dreams I have where I am flying."

"Look north. Those peaks are the Sierras. They're about a hundred miles away.

"The air is so clear up here." She hummed.

"What's that tune? It's nice."

"Oh, I didn't know I was humming. That's the melody I hear when I have happy flying dreams."

Ahead, a rotor cloud was forming, looking like a giant five-mile long roll of fluffy cotton.

"What's that ahead?"

"That's a rotor cloud I told you about. It forms right at the edge of where the air is going up.

Wispy fingers of mist broke off from the roll, streamed upward like waterfalls, for a thousand feet. Rainbows appeared sparkling in the sun. In a few minutes, we were flying along the edge of the cloud.

Raven readjusted her shoulder harness. "This is magical! The silence! We are skimming along something that looks like Niagara Falls, turned upside down. Almost a transcendent experience."

When I steered the sailplane to where a wingtip trailed in the mist, the sailplane rumbled.

"What's that?"

"The rotor is telling us not to come in there." I steered clear.

"Can we just fly in the smooth, friendly air for a while."

"Yes"

I reached forward and put my hand on Raven's shoulder. Raven placed her hand on mine.

We flew for several minutes and then the sailplane shuddered.

I made a few turns. " I think we have to head back. We're at the end of the wave. We're about as high as we should go without oxygen, and we don't want to get up to where the airliners fly."

"You mean there could be airliners here?"

"No, air traffic control routes them away from here on wave days"

I reversed course and got into the smooth air, I returned my hand to Raven's shoulder. Her hand returned to mine. We silently absorbed the spectacular experience, riding the wave of air and the wave of joy.

A half hour later, I flew to where we could drop out of the bottom of the wave and back to the field.

Raven only held onto the cockpit handle for a short time. "That wasn't so bad."

We approached the runway. I looked at the windsock flying above the operations trailer. "See it is calm down here." That's a relief.

Raven straightened up from her scrunched posture. "I guess we know where the real action is."

We rolled to a stop in the sailplane tie-down area. I opened the canopy. We sat in silence for a minute.

"That was amazing!" Raven unbuckled her harness. "It started like a roller coaster ride without the screaming. Then it turned into a spiritual experience."

We climbed out onto the tarmac. Without a word Raven gave me a big hug, held me. "Thank you, I'll never forget that.

"Me neither." *The love energy between us was strong.*

Raven looked at me with concern. "But now I have to visit the ladies' room."

"After I tie this glider down I'll walk down to check out my sailplane trailer. I'll meet you there."

I felt uneasy. *Something is wrong at my sailplane trailer.* I closed my eyes and saw, in a visualization, the vague outline of something scratched in the ground. I hurried to the trailer, and there it was. A hieroglyphic symbol was scratched under the back, the same symbol I saw Candice's windshield in the parking garage. I took out my cell phone and took several pictures of it. Then I opened the access door. Nothing seemed to be disturbed. I checked the access door on the other end where everything also seemed normal. *There might be fingerprints,* I thought. When I looked, I could see the normal desert dust grime around the doors was wiped clean. *I'll let Danae's security people know about this tomorrow*

Raven walked up. "Picnic time!"

A cold breeze stirred my hair. "We need a sheltered place for our picnic, the wind is starting to come down here. We could go over to the patio behind my place."

Raven dropped her eyes. "Not today, let's go somewhere out in nature."

"Okay. I know just the place."

We went back to the airport office.I paid my bill and wrote a note requesting the staff to inform me if Mr. male Caucasian five-five stocky build gray crew cut gold-rimmed glasses showed up again.

"What was that about?"

"I'll tell you at lunch."

We drove up a dirt road alongside the airfield to the end and then turned uphill on another steep, rough dirt and desert rock road. We came to ruins of a building. Only two stacked river stone walls of a barn remained, with an open side facing the desert to the north.. We went inside where the walls sheltered us from the wind. The sun was warm. A clean, but weatherworn picnic table sat near the wall.

I explained that a glider pilot I knew had cleaned the place up and used it as a place to park his RV when he came to fly.

"What a beautiful view," said Raven.

Looking away from the mountains toward the Sierras, we could see the clouds were broken, and the spotty sunlight was illuminating patches of desert. The clouds moved; the desert seemed engulfed by waves of light and dark.

"Why is this here?" asked Raven. "What is the story behind this old ruin?"

"Almost a century ago, there was a socialist utopian-driven dream of building a planned city here. Farming was possible because there was more rainfall then. The colony fell apart within a few years. Their brand of socialism shared everything, including wives. Way down there, at the bottom of this ridge, there are still olive trees, which have survived from that era."

"I wondered abut those poor old desiccated trees as we drove by. The energy at this spot is good. Must be happy cow energy."

She glanced at me, expecting she had gone somewhere she shouldn't.

"You're right.

Raven looked surprised. "I thought you didn't believe in energies and things like that."

"It doesn't bother me so much now. If it is okay for me to have visions of car wrecks, it is okay for you to sense the energy of happy people and happy cows here."

"I'm sorry I didn't pack any milk to drink. We'll only have coffee today." Raven unpacked the picnic basket. She gave me a mysterious smile I didn't understand as she took off her down jacket.

Today, she had a different table setting. The tablecloth was blue and white checked, and the plastic plates were white. The tumblers were stainless steel and said Starbucks on the side. She set out a crystal dish of olives, celery, small tomatoes and radishes, and then unwrapped sandwiches.

"I was thinking as we drove up here that I could write a narrative of the wave flight, all the turbulence, then the beauty, the potential danger lurking a few feet away, then more turbulence, and then a glide to a smooth landing. Then I could give it to my high school students and ask them to use that as a metaphor to write a story about people interacting, the ups and downs of teen dating, and getting tied down to a safe spot."

I continued the thought. "I had never thought about wave flying as a metaphor. I've had some turbulent relationships.

Lately, my life hasn't been ups and downs so much. It's more like the overcast clouds of my life are unzipping, exposing a whole new blue sky of something I don't understand, and which I need to explore."

Without saying anything, Raven reached into the picnic basket pulled out a magic marker and a napkin, and wrote something on it. She pushed it across the table, put her chin on her hand, and looked at me with her impish grin. I looked at the paper. She smiled. On the paper was a big "A+."

"Thanks." I returned her smile. "Oh, I almost forgot to mention, I had a premonition that proved to be true today. Before I went to check on my sailplane trailer, I had a great feeling of uneasiness and had a visualization of seeing something scratched in the ground. When I got there, I saw something that alarmed me, a mystical symbol scratched in the in the sand."

I pulled out my cell phone and showed Raven the picture of the symbol.

She looked. "That just looks like graffiti. Why are you concerned?"

"That symbol appeared on the car windshield of one of my key witness while she was in my office. I sent a photo of it to Danae at the Colson Foundation. She is having their security consultants check it out."

"Premonition, okay, extra credit for that." She nodded then added raised eyebrows to her grin.

"This has been a wonderful day. But I have to be back early tonight because tomorrow I have to correct papers and do grades. Maybe we should stop by your place to let me freshen up."

I reached into my down parka pocket and got the Snickers bar I bought from the vending machine.

She grinned. "More extra credit. You read my mind."

I felt that mysterious energy around my heart again.

Monday, as I entered my office, Zaza greeted me with a slight smile. "He has that look about him again. The desert flowers must be in bloom. Weekends, it must be Flopsey. No! I can't keep track. Flowers in order?"

I ignored her. "I'm going to go to Rocky Butte for a court date on Thursday at nine o'clock and to interview Steve Manteo. Please make reservations for me to fly to Sacramento on Wednesday, arriving there in the morning if possible. Rent me a car, and make a reservation at some motel in Rocky Butte for one night. I'll be in court there on Thursday morning. I'll drive out to Steve's in the afternoon. I'll play it by ear about where I'll stay Thursday night. Book a flight back to L.A. in the early morning on Friday."

"Got it! Danae Hamilton called and said she's coming in tomorrow morning at nine, only for a half hour. She doesn't want a formal progress report. She wants to discuss security issues about the trial."

I spent the rest of the day in the office preparing my case.

The next morning Zaza buzzed me. "Danae Hamilton just arrived. She's in the conference room."

I put on my coat and hurried to meet her

"Good morning Dave, "Danae thrust her hand out for a handshake. "How is the trial preparation going? Are you getting comfortable with the subject?"

Danae was wearing a navy blue business suit with a light yellow scarf tied around her neck. She was giving me her icy stare, and I knew I was being 'read.' In a few seconds, her face relaxed and seemed friendly.

"Good to see you Danae. I'm now comfortable with these new ideas. Dr. Montgomery was very helpful. I have a court date in Rocky Butte Thursday, and I'll meet with Steve Manteo that evening and stay over as needed."

Danae gave me one of her highly-practiced professional smiles.

"We can talk about that later. I'm sure you have it under control. There are security issues we need to address. Our consultants have been talking to your Mr. Steel and have done some further investigations. It appears the trial has attracted a group of people we should be concerned about. They call themselves Skeptemos and claim to be part of a secret organization that has existed since the Renaissance. Their mission is to stamp out bad science. They like to go after anything of a psychic nature.

"Is this the Skeptics organization I have hear of?"

"No. There are legitimate organizations, like the Skeptics. They are reputable scientific people that make it their business to debunk all psychic phenomena. These are not the same guys.

"Skeptemos members seem to be more like the nerds that get addicted to video games and go to game conventions wearing tights or capes. From our reports, Skeptemos people have a mission to save the world. They believe that there is a conspiracy to destroy science so that evil people can take over with superstition and fear. The 'secret' order doesn't seem to have existed more than a few years."

I shook my head. "They sound like crazies. Are they dangerous? Assassins? Terrorists?"

"I don't know. Our security firm traced the ownership of the tracking device on your car to a person who has a website that touts the Skeptemos line. He is a retired Army explosive ordnance disposal specialists and fits the description of the man Dr. Montgomery saw near her car and was reported being at CeystalSky airport. He could be dangerous.

"Our security firm suggests that we rent a place outside Rocky Butte for the duration of the trial. Then, people come and go unnoticed. An isolated place will make security easier. I'll take care of the arrangements."

"Sounds good, I'll defer to your judgment. I'm going up there next week for a court date and to visit Steve Manteo. I'll hang around town and get a feel for the place. I was raised in a small logging town in Northern California and understand life in small towns. Everyone knows what everyone else is doing, and the rumor hotline is faster than the speed of light."It might be wise to put a local on the security payroll, who'd know about all the rumors, and could tell you the business of strangers in town."

"I'll suggest that to our security consultants. Now, I need to get going."

I walked Danae to the lobby and shook hands with her. "Thank you for selecting Bracken and Stevens to represent you in this matter. This is a good change of subject and I find that I have become excited investigating it."

Danae looked at me without blinking (I was being 'read' again) then smiled her professional smile. "We're very pleased with our selection."

I walked her to the elevator and said goodbye. As I walked back into the lobby, Carolyn gave me her 'You are such a wonderful man' smile, and I gave her my 'thanks for being a polite receptionist' smile.

9

ROCKY BUTTE

I drove into Rocky Butte late on Wednesday afternoon. A bridge bearing the date 1934 spanned Butte Creek. The stream swelled with the spring snowmelt runoff. A blue sign read *Rocky Butte, population 670*. I saw what I'd expected: small town America, little changed from the 1950s. It had one main street and one cross street. A liquor store advertised 'bait' in its window. The River View and Rocky Butte Inn motels sat next to a hardware store that advertised "Gold Pans and Mining Supplies" and "Satellite Dishes." One of the two restaurants had a neon sign in the window that read "Eat." A dozen other businesses formed the downtown at the next intersection.

It was quiet. Only the saloons, The Claim Jumper, and The Diggings were busy. Pickups filled the parking lot in front. Some of the rusty trucks looked to be from the 1950s. There was a school on the outskirts of the town. A Tasty Freeze marking the edge of town had a service window with shaded parking area in the back. Two teenagers sat and ate soft cones at a picnic bench. I headed back to the center of town and turned onto the only cross street, identified only as Highway 32. The Butte News was on the next block across from Courthouse Square. A white Greek Revival style courthouse dominated the Square. A granite staircase led up to the second story entrance guarded by a colonnade of four two-story columns supporting a triangular roof. The facade had 1922 engraved in bold Roman letters. A plain, undated office annex was grafted on the back. A separate entrance in the annex had *Sheriff's Substation* painted on the door. A patrol car parked in front.

A two-story-high red brick library sat on one corner of Courthouse Square. It looked to be from the era of the 1920s when Carnegie built libraries. A Pioneer Museum with an adjacent park with picnic tables took up another corner. An old locomotive from a logging train stood by a granite slab engraved with eighteen names of those killed in "The Earthquake of 1872."

It didn't take long to tour Rocky Butte.

My first stop was a half mile out of town at the Sodastroms', the parents of Lucy. They lived in a small white house surrounded by pine trees with an unpaved driveway to a garage in the back. A dark brown mare, I guessed it had been Lucy's, grazed on the spring grass in a corral by a barn.

Ann Sodastrom met me at the door, and I introduced myself. She was skinny and looked as though she had lost more weight than she should. Her print housedress hung on her. Ed, who was sitting in a recliner watching TV, got up. He was also lean, with a hollow look to his face and stooped shoulders. Their grief was clear. They didn't need to discuss the case.

I introduced myself and gave them assurances that their trial would be over soon. We made small talk until they were comfortable with me. They told me which church they attended, and their favorite things about Rocky Butte. They said they were native Californians and spent most of their lives in Sacramento. They brightened as they talked about themselves.

Ed will make a touching witness.

Bob's Cafe on Main Street looked good for dinner and gossip. I sat on a swiveling stool at the counter that gave me the full smell the greasy cooking going on behind the pass-trough window. The only other customer was a man with a white beard sitting in a booth reading a paper.

The waitress sauntered up, looked me over, "What'll-y-have?"

She was approaching fifty, gray-haired, wearing a pink, starched uniform that included a tiara-like hat. She had a name badge that read Agnes.

I haven't seen a waitress dressed like this since high school

"Can I see a dinner menu?"

"Same menu one all day, honey, special tonight is pork chops."

"Then, I'll order the special."

I looked at the bottom of the menu where it read, "Free Wi-Fi for customers."

"You have Wi-Fi."

"We're up-to-date around here. We even have cell phone service so visitors can stay connected. Do you live near?"

"No, I have business at the courthouse tomorrow, and then I plan on visiting someone up the hill."

"If you're trying to beat a speeding ticket, forget it. Judge Jeremiah Cartwright–we call him 'The Hangin' Judge,'–don't have much tolerance for speeders. You might end up spending the night in jail."

"Where's it?"

"It's over in the basement of the annex at the courthouse, behind the sheriff substation. The main county jail is up in Pine Mountain where the county sheriff has his office. They need it up there with all the tourists and skiers."

"I'll try to keep out of both places. How long have you lived here, Agnes?"

"My whole my life. My great-grandfather worked a mining claim here. I grew up on a farm in the valley. My roots are here."

In a few minutes, she brought me dinner.

"You must be the fellow from L.A. that is staying over at the River View Motel."

In this slow season before the vacationers arrive, everything is news. I'd guess everyone in town knows of my motel reservation. Lesson number one. I'll be a center of attention while I am here.

"That's right. I'd better get over there and check in. I'll be back for breakfast, Agnes."

I could tell I was being watched. From my car, I saw Agnes on her cell phone.

This town is like a police state, except the tyranny comes from the rule of boredom. The trial will give them something to talk about.

After dinner, I enjoyed a walk in the fine Sierra evening. The late-day yellow sunlight made the green of the pine trees glow as I walked through the woods on a game trail. The forest was quiet, birds were having their evening rest, and it was still. I smelled the pines and kicked the cones lying in the yellow dirt. Butte Creek was rushing with the early summer snow melt. The trail led to the Creek bank. An eddy in the water caused by a fallen tree swirled out a pool. Small fish darted in and out of the shadows. The bottom of the pool sparkled with polished, water-worn pebbles.

I'd bet Raven would like this. My life has changed. If this were one of my normal patent cases, I'd be in a city hotel room preparing legal arguments or sitting in a bar looking into a whiskey glass, hoping to find an interesting woman stranger wanting company. Now, I'm looking into a creek in a mountain town wishing for the company of an interesting woman I know.

Back at the River View Motel, I sat in a lawn chair, watched the sunset.

My life is going in a direction I didn't plan. I'm a mainstream science guy. Now, I'm immersed in obscure ideas of remote viewing and clairvoyance. My reputation as a scientific lawyer may be in a precarious position. It's strange. These new things are feeling comfortable.

I watched the sky grow dark, and then I said, "Good evening Hesperus."

On the drive to court, I had an idea. Why not introduce false signals into the gossip grapevine? I stopped by the hardware store. Inside, a middle-aged woman watched me as though I was shoplifting. *Agnes must have called her.* Two plastic gold-panning pans and a glass vial were what I needed today. I paid for them and wondered what the grapevine would report.

The early morning sunlight made the granite steps of the courthouse sparkle, At the top of the stairs, I stopped, turned around and looked out onto the square. *This place has a different feel than the other courthouses. There is a solemnity instead of the usual hustle and bustle.*

Wait! Is that a psychic observation?

I entered the courtroom, sat in the third row, and waited for the session to begin. The clerk called the court to order and announced the judge.

Judge Cartwright appeared, a short, balding, obese man in his sixties, with a jowly face that reminded me of cartoon bears. When he spoke I knew he was no Yogi Bear: he was firm, and his presence emanated control. Mine was the third case on the docket, following DUI and disturbing the peace hearings. The bailiff called my case, and I stepped forward, filed my papers, and made the customary motions. After the defense had done the same, the judge recessed the court and asked us to join him in his chambers.

I introduced myself to defense counsel. Dean Buttress was a slight man with a bald pate. He combed his hair over the top from the side. His puffy face made me think he might be an alcoholic. A Hitler-style mustache wiggled in a funny way when he talked.

In his chambers, the judge was very abrupt. "I don't want you big city lawyers turning this trial into a circus. Don't give any interviews to the media before or during the trial. Our economy depends on vacationing families, and we can't have Rocky Butte getting a reputation as a place where people lose children. People around here make their living in the summers and will be burdened by jury duty. So, I'm fast-tracking this case to get it over by the beginning of the tourist season. I'm scheduling you for one month from today. Any objections.?"

"No."

"None your honor."

"Then, I'll welcome you back in one month. Remember, I want no pre-trial publicity. I can take care of the Butte News. Thank you, gentlemen." The judge rose, and we both hurried out of chambers.

I turned to exchange pleasantries with Mr. Buttress. He walked away.

I drove to Bob's Cafe for a cup of coffee before I made the trip up the hill to Steve Manteo's. Agnes greeted me with a big smile as though I were a local now.

"Coffee?"

"Yes," I sat on the same stool. "I didn't get sent to jail."

"I put in a good word for you," Agnes smiled.

A cowboy hat-wearing man in a rusty pickup drove up and parked in front of the restaurant. As he came in he said, "Agnes, I just came across the creek bridge and guess what? Downstream, on the motel side, where that fallen tree is. Otis Wilson and Bud Johnson are panning for gold. That claim belonged to old man Williams, and he gave up on it years ago."

This town has a well-connected gossip network. Since I bought gold pans and been seen sitting by a creek, I must have found gold.

The next morning I drove toward Steve Manteo's place, passing Courthouse Square, and admiring the few scattered homes that gave way to the forest. I stopped by the Sodastrom's house to tell them the schedule. Ed Sodastrom said, "I'm glad it will soon be done. The prospect of a trial is taking a toll."

"I am sure that Judge Cartwright will make it short. He won't allow any nonsense in the testimony."

I came to the now-closed Rawhide Cafe fifteen miles out of town on a winding mountain road. This was the Sheriff's search and rescue headquarters when they'd searched for Lucy. It was an old-fashioned roadside diner with a counter and a row of booths along one side. A hand-lettered sign in the window read *Closed Until Memorial Day.* An abandoned two-pump gas station was nest to the cafe. Dusty signs in the window said 'Fishing Gear' and, 'Beer and Wine.' It now was an office with a desk and file cabinets.

A few miles beyond the Rawhide Cafe my GPS directed me onto an unmarked dirt road, which led up the mountain and then onto an unmarked dirt driveway. The navigator announced, "You have arrived."

Steve's house was a log cabin, the kind made from brown-stained factory logs. It perched on a hillside and had a spacious deck on the front, a steep roof, and a satellite dish mounted on the peak.

Steve appeared at the rail. "Come on up."

I walked up the two flights of stairs and was greeted by Steve, a six-foot-two bear of a man who looked like an NFL lineman. He had a well-tanned face and sparkling blue eyes. A woman came out onto the deck carrying a tray with glasses of iced tea. Steve introduced me to his wife, Georgia, a striking Latina-looking woman, with shiny long straight-black hair, large brown eyes, and thick eyebrows.

"Beautiful view." I took a glass.

The three of us sat at a picnic table on the deck and talked about Rocky Butte, the people there, and the aesthetic virtues of living away from civilization. I told them of my home in the desert.

Georgia commented as she looked at me, or rather through me, "I pick up the mental picture of a dark-complexioned lady with black hair and brown eyes." She paused, then added, "and a love for a desert place."

"Georgia, don't scare the man!" Steve chuckled.

"No, I'm felling at home with ESP and the people who have it!" I smiled at Georgia. "Her name is Raven, and she spends time with me. She has some psychic powers."

I paused and had thoughts of Raven.

"Before this case, I never thought about ESP. I know I can read juries and tell when I'm going in the wrong direction in an argument, or when something is upsetting or confusing. I always called it intuition."

Steve nodded toward Georgia, "She is much better than me at reading other people's mental pictures. But, she doesn't do remote viewing well. We all have our unique abilities."

Georgia's eyes looked through or past me for a second; then she smiled a knowing smile. "I'll fix lunch while you guys talk. We insist that you stay for dinner and spend the night in our guest cabin up the hill. It isn't much, but the solitude is great."

"Thank you. I'm delighted to stay for dinner, but I have to get back to Sacramento tonight to catch an early plane tomorrow. Since the judge only gave me a month to prepare for the trial, I need office time."

Steve smiled and began, "I'd better discuss what you came to learn. Most people have a surprising amount of unacknowledged ESP ability. When they first started the remote viewing experiments at SRI, in 1972, they hired recognized psychics or clairvoyants, people tested in laboratories or were known professionally as 'psychics.' One day, they tried a remote viewing experiment using our project secretary. Although she had never taken part in any paranormal activity, she did well and surprised everyone. After that, they developed a training program to use ordinary people who showed aptitude in tests. They recruited me because I excelled in experiments done in our Psych One class at Stanford."

"I read that in your book."

"Good! I won't have to tell those stories again. Where would you like to start?"

"Explain the basic process of remote viewing."

"Many people experience unexpected psychic events. "Mothers will sense their child is in trouble and rescue them from a perilous situation. A person will decide not to board an airliner that later crashes. Drivers will take a different route to work on a day when a horrific auto accident happens on their usual route.

"Many people call this 'intuition' or 'clairvoyance.'"

I was getting confused. "Tell me what 'clairvoyant' means."

"I use this limited definition: the power to sense features of objects or feel the emotions of people in another space or time.

"I spent years doing clairvoyant tasks for the CIA. They gave me a target or objective, and I'd go into an extended deep meditation and sensed basic things about the target. For instance, if they wanted to know what was going on in a building photographed by a spy satellite, they'd show me the picture or give me the geographic coordinates. I would go into a deep meditation and sense what someone inside the building might observe. It might be noises, colors, shapes, nature of objects, maybe something big like a ship hull, or level of activity, such as busy or quiet. Over time, often a period of hours, I'd continue to sense the nature of what people might be doing. Sometimes, but not always, I'd get an image of the place. While I was in deep meditation, I'd dictate my observations to an assistant who guided me toward gaining more detail."

"So this wasn't a flash process, like the mother sensing her child was in trouble?"

"Sometimes yes but most times no. I think when I'm remote viewing, I'm getting the information from a person who is physically at the target. If that person is a 'good sender,' or involved in the activity, I receive a lot of information. If the only person there is a half-asleep guard, I don't get a lot."

"Can you give me some examples?"

"No. The program gave the CIA tons of data, much of which verified by other sources such as satellites or on-the-ground spies. All I can say is that it was successful. Two presidents were briefed on data from the program. I don't think examples in those dark files will ever be public. The twenty years the funding of the program received is the greatest testament to the success."

"The photo of The President awarding you a medal is in the book. I read the citation. That award speaks of success."

"I wish I could tell you the story that led to being considered for that medal. It was a triumphant event."

"What could we use in the trial to give you credibility? I don't think showing them a picture of you and The President will be enough."

"I can get you television footage. I used to do a 'circus act' of remote sensing for TV shows."

"What did you do?"

"I'd describe photographs in sealed envelopes. Somebody associated with a TV show, who did not know me, would collect a few eight-by-ten-inch pictures of landmarks in the city and seal them in unlabeled envelopes. During the broadcast, the host of the show would pick one, and I'd describe the picture inside."

"I'd love to show something like that to the jury."

"Do you still do these demonstrations?"

"No. I now have paying clients. In the past decade, I've been remote viewing as a consultant for a variety of individuals, companies, and law enforcement agencies."

"Could we get a client to testify?"

"I'm afraid not. I require a confidentiality agreement with my customers that has very strict nondisclosure provisions. I agree that I will never disclose either their names or their interests; they agree that they will never disclose that I am the source of information, or that I've been in their employ. The arrangement avoids embarrassing situations and protects my privacy. I've produced spectacular results for people, but I can't disclose them."

"Do you need a disclosure agreement from me?"

"No! I consider this a public service, giving the Sheriff his comeuppance. I have to warn you I will hide behind my disclosure agreements if you ask any questions about my confidential or classified activities."

"Thanks, I'll respect that and object if opposing counsel asks questions of that sort.

"I have to decide what to give a jury of lay people. I can't give them stuff that is too spooky or stuff that is too technical. I'll sort that out in the next few days. Tell me about the night Lucy died."

Steve's mood grew somber. I could tell this was a painful subject for him. He began, "I was driving back from

Sacramento. It was dark, around 8:30, when I came to the Rawhide Cafe, There was a light snow falling."

"I noticed the cafe on the way up here," I added.

"It was lit up by headlights of patrol cars. Red lights were flashing everywhere. The Sheriff's command center van was in the parking lot with a generator running. I could hear radios chatting. Two deputies stood guard at the footbridge over Bear Creek behind the cafe. Paramedics stood by an ambulance. Many other people were standing around, one person with a tracking dogs people in orange vests and backpacks with rope and rescue equipment. I parked and walked to the Cafe. The Sheriff and several other people were inside the cafe arguing in front of a map hung on the wall. It was a very busy place.

"I walked up to the deputy guarding the door and said, 'I needed to speak with the Sheriff. I can help. I am psychic.'

He blew me off saying, "He is too busy to talk to the public."

"I hurried back to my car and got a copy of my book–the one you read–and what I call my credentials folder. It contains a picture of The President and me, letters of commendation from government people, news clippings of me helping find lost people, and letters of commendation for working with police in solving missing person cases."

I looked at Steve. "Can I show that to the jury at the trial?"

"Yes."

"Please go on."

"I showed the book and folder to the deputy who examined it for a while and then led me to Sheriff Bogend. He was sweating despite the cold and mumbling to himself. I showed him my book and credentials folder. He thumbed through them without looking at them and handed them back without speaking to me. He shouted at the deputy, 'Damn it, why are you wasting my time with fortunetellers. We have a lost child to find. Get him out of here!'

"The deputy, smarting from being chastised, showed me to the door and said, 'Thank you, we don't need your services.' Then he whispered, 'I apologize for how he treated you. The Sheriff is stressed out over getting everything organized.'

"Men wearing orange search and rescue jackets were passing a photo around. I asked to see it. While looking at the picture, a psychic connection with Lucy formed. I knew exactly where she was. She had found shelter under some logs and was crying and cold. It was vivid.

"My anger rose while walking back to the cafe. I pushed the deputy aside and walked over to the map and drew an X on the map where they would find Lucy."

"Stop right there," commanded the Sheriff with his hand on his holster.

"She is here where the X is, about a hundred yards up Bear Creek from that old logging trestle," I shouted. "In a shelter but is cold. She may not have much more time."

"The Sheriff bellowed, 'We've found her tracks in the snow going in another direction. Get Houdini out of here! If you come around here again, I'll arrest you for obstructing officers in an investigation. Don't go hunting for her. You'll be destroying her trail for the trackers.'

"The deputy grabbed my arm and walked me out of the cafe.

"I walked up to one of the men wearing an orange vest and said. 'Can't anyone do anything? She is on the other side of Bear Creek down about a half mile in a log shelter. I'd risk the Sheriff's wrath and go myself if I could get across the creek.'"

"Sir, we can't do that. By law, The Sheriff as Incident Commander has the sole power to make decisions on this Search and Rescue operation. You will have to talk to him."

"He threw me out!"

"We're sorry sir, we can't violate the legal chain of command."

"I walked around to the back of the cafe and spoke to the two officers guarding the bridge. 'I have to get to the other side of the creek. The girl's life is at stake.' I tried to push through and found my arms pinned behind me. The officer said, 'Sir, I don't want to handcuff and arrest you. Only personnel authorized by the sheriff can pass.'"

Steve was almost in tears and had trouble finishing the story.

"I barely made it home because I was so occupied sensing Lucy's distress. I couldn't sleep because of my concern. About midnight, she died, and I fell to sleep."

I was quiet while Steve sat deep in thought.

Georgia came out onto the deck, using her hip to push the screen door open while carrying a large tray loaded with sandwiches and iced tea.

She looked at Steve. "You told him the story of that night." She walked over, kissed him on the forehead, and said, "It's difficult for him to relate that story."

I shook my head. "I think the Colson Foundation wants to make sure nobody else has to tell similar stories."

Steve got up, took a glass of iced tea from the table and raised it in a toast, "I'll drink to that."

Over lunch, we chatted about living in the mountains and desert, the wildlife, and the aesthetics of such a life. I told them being raised in the woods in a small northern California logging town, and how my home-town gossip grapevine worked as it did in Rocky Butte.

"Your description of the sensing process may be needed in the trial." I paused for a second to think. "The jury needs to have a general understanding of how remote viewing works. My client, the Colson foundation, wants me to introduce scientific data into the trial to provide precedents for future trials. Are you familiar with the mathematician Candice Montgomery's work on eight-dimensional space?"

Steve shook his head. "I'm not an expert on mathematical subjects. Her thesis sounds good. I have to say: birds don't need ornithology or aerodynamics to fly; they simply do it. People doing remote viewing don't need an eight-dimensional space theory. We believe in the phenomenon because of our personal experience. We are not the audience for Dr. Montgomery's papers."

I paused for a minute. "I need to introduce enough science in the trial to refute any experts they might produce who'd testify 'there is no scientific evidence proving that remote viewing is real.' The jury doesn't need to understand the theory. They only have to believe Dr. Montgomery is a knowledgeable expert. It's important to have the scientific viewpoint on the record for reference in other trials."

"I can understand that. For the trial, I suggest that you have me do a live demonstration of remote viewing. You design it after you look at the videos. Don't prep me on what you decide. Then, I can testify that we haven't prearranged a rigged experiment."

Georgia interrupted. "It's now time for our afternoon nap and meditation. Let's adjourn until five. Dave, go up to the guest cottage and rest, or enjoy the view."

I walked up a steep hill to a one-room log cabin with a porch. It had a spectacular view of the valley. I settled into one of the soft deck chairs and closed my eyes. My thoughts turned to Raven. I sensed she was in a noisy classroom. *Is this remote viewing?* I dozed off.

At five, I walked back to the main house and found Georgia setting the table on the deck for dinner.

"Did you have a nap?"

"Yes, I sat and snoozed in the sun."

"After the trial is over, why don't you return and spend a day or two relaxing? She smiled a knowing smile. "Bring that black-haired lady with the brown eyes. I'd love to meet her."

"I'll do that."

"And, Steve is a legally ordained minister. If you're in need of that service," she added without looking up.

Steve came out onto the deck and dropped into a chair looking blurry-eyed. Georgia poured a cup of tea from a pot on the table and handed to him.

"Excuse me," Steve rubbed his eyes. "I'm not back yet."

Georgia put her hand on his shoulder. "Dave said he would come back and spend time after the trial and bring his friend with him."

"Wonderful! We can go on hikes and experience the beauty of this country. In my business, I spend many hours in meditation; I need to ground myself in a place like this to keep balanced. When I worked in Palo Alto, we lived in a cabin between Palo Alto and the ocean. I couldn't have survived without my daily nature fix."

After dinner, Steve asked, "Do you want to know in advance how the trial will turn out?"

"I'm not sure. It might spoil the fun."

"I'll mail you the 'win/no win' prediction of the verdict in a sealed envelope in a few days. You can open it before or after the trial."

"How will you make such a prediction?"

"Do you see that stump by the driveway? On the morning after the verdict, I will stand on it and hold either of two things: that long-handled pick ax over there if the verdict was in your favor, or the wet rag-cloth mop in the kitchen if you lost the case. I will place my hands on the ax head or the wet mop. I commit to a future reality where I'll do either of those things on the morning after the trial is over.

"Tomorrow, I'll go into meditation and synchronize my mind with my future self, standing here on the stump the day after the trial. I'll concentrate on the sensory information I'll experience in that future. If I get 'firm, sharp, metal, dangerous, wood handle, rusty, etc.' I'll know you won. If the sensory information is 'soft, cloth, limp, cotton, wet, etc.,' I'll know you lost. I'm good at this kind of prediction."

I let the idea in. "If you tell me I won, and I relax in preparing the case, I might lose. Isn't that altering the outcome?"

"No. It might alter how or why you win the case, but you will still win the case. That's the way it works." Steve shrugged.

I thought for a minute. "Send me the prediction, and I'll choose when to read it." *I'm not sure I believe this. I guess I have to see him in action.*

By this time, Steve and Georgia were like old friends. I said I must leave, and we exchanged warm hugs, Hugs aren't my normal way of saying goodbye to potential witnesses.

I'll stop at Bob's Cafe to act like a local. I'll give Agnes something to put on the gossip grapevine.

I was careful to sit at the same rotating stool at the counter.

Agnes came over. "What'll-y-have?" This time, she had a slight smile of recognition.

"Just coffee."

"Ya-got-it."

The cafe was empty except for a booth of three gray-haired men, wearing their Stetson hats as they ate. One was looking me over.

"What do you think of Rocky Butte so far?" Agnes eyed me.

"I'm from a little logging town in northern California. I like small towns."

"Did your friend find you? He was in here yesterday asking where you might be. I sent him to the courthouse. Millie, the clerk over there, said he wanted to look at stuff on your court case."

"What did he look like?"

"He had a stocky build, like a farmhand, gray crew cut hair, round gold wire-rimmed glasses. Millie said you have a case against Sheriff Bogend for roughing up someone. Bogend is a real bastard. I hope you fix him. He often hassles people around here. He's not much of a tipper, either."

"I don't know him. He must be an insurance investigator.

The judge isn't giving me much time before he hears the case. I might rent a place up here. Are there vacation rental homes available?"

"Lots. Most of them are managed by agencies in Pine Mountain. There are several dude ranches around here. Are you going to bring your family up with you?"

"No, I'm unattached and will be alone enjoying the solitude and being away from L.A."

"Find time to pan for gold and meet local gals. People are panning again because of the current gold price." Agnes stared at me.

She wants to check if my expression changed at the mention of gold. I'll play her game. I raised my eyebrows and smiled. "Isn't that great!"

"I'll introduce you to a widow woman who's a friend of mine."

"I might try prospecting for both women and gold if I have the time. I'll be working at my desk getting ready for the trial. You'll have me coming in here for your dinner special."

I looked at my watch. "Good coffee, I'd better get going."

As I drove away, I saw Agnes on her cell phone. At the edge of town, I stopped the car and emailed Danae. It read, "The man from Skeptemos was in Rocky Butte inquiring about me and visiting the courthouse. I met with the Sodastroms and Steve Manteo. Now returning to L.A."

10

BACK IN LA

Monday morning, I was back at my office. In the lobby, Carolyn looked disheveled. She didn't even greet me. A small overnight bag sat behind her desk. "I'm available for the weekend," hadn't worked out as expected.

Zaza greeted me with, "Well, if it isn't the mountain man! How was rabbit hunting in Rocky Butte? I've heard stories about those Sierra mining towns. Meet any dance-hall girls?"

"All business. There is gourmet dining at Bob's Cafe. Here, I brought you a gold pan."

"A pretty yellow one! I wanted one of these. Irving needs a new hobby. I've been trying to get him away from the television."

"How was your weekend?" I asked.

"Irving watched TV. Period. You had a call from someone named Dan at CrystalSky." She handed me a slip of paper with his phone number on it.

"He's one of the tow pilots there. I hope nothing happened to my sailplane."

I called Dan, and he explained, "Dave, I don't know what this means, but you remember that funny guy with the gray crew cut and gold-rimmed glasses that checked out your sailplane trailer?"

"Yes, the one you described the day I flew the wave."

"The other day," Dan continued, "I flew up to the soaring operation on Ogden to deliver a tow plane that had been here for an overhaul. I saw Charlie Sears from Santa Fe assembling his sailplane. You remember him from the regional contest we had here at CrystalSky last year?"

"Yes, I talked to Charlie during the contest. How's he doing?"

"He was spending a week flying at Ogden. He was taking his bird out of the trailer and putting it together. The funny guy with the gray crew cut who was here at CrystalSky was helping him. While I talked to Charlie I got a good look at the guy. He was uptight, like a Marine on guard duty. I couldn't figure out why he was there. You might give Charlie a call and find out what the guy's story is."

"I will. I have Charlie's cell phone number. Thanks. Call me if you the stranger shows up again."

I called Charlie and told him that Dan had said he'd seen him in Ogden. We chatted about flying and Ogden weather and soaring conditions.

Charlie said, "I've heard Ingo Dorner is now flying in your area of the Mojave? How is it to have a world champion in your midst? Do you ever meet him?"

"I've only seen his sailplane from a distance in the mountains near CrystalSky. He flies out of an airport ten miles from there. I met him once at a pilot's briefing at a soaring contest. His mere presence intimidated the whole room. He's a scary guy!"

I then asked Charlie about the man Dan saw helping assemble the sailplane.

"I'd never seen the man before. He was just standing around, so I asked him if he would help put the wings on. He was very interested in how everything pieced together, as though he were a mechanical engineer, but he didn't know anything about flying. After we had finished, he drove off in his white van."

"Did you find out where he was from, or what he was doing there?"

"No, he wasn't a very personable guy. Why the interest?"

"Dan observed him hanging around my glider trailer at CrystalSky. He thought he looked suspicious. Dan said he'd seen him with you in Ogden so I thought I'd find out what you know about him."

Charlie continued, "I think 'suspicious' is a good description of him. Maybe 'creepy' is better."

I thanked Charlie and told him of my wave flight before we said our goodbyes.

I emailed a report of the Skeptemos' guy's interest in sailplanes to Colson's security consultant, EB Services.

Zaza buzzed me and said, "Bracken is here this morning and wants an update on the case. Shall I see if he's free?"

"Yes."

After a short call, Zaza buzzed me back and said, "Okay to go up there now."

As I walked in, Phil motioned me to sit in a chair in front of his desk.

"How is Sodastrom shaping up?"

"The judge set a trial date to twenty-eight days from now. He warned me against any pre-trial publicity. He doesn't want the tourist town of Rocky Butte to be publicized as a place unsafe for families. The county counsel lawyer, who will defend the County, didn't impress me."

Phil glanced at the calendar on his iPhone. "Will that give you enough time to prepare? Isn't there too much science for you to assimilate in a month?"

"Fortunately, Colson has done the work for me. He has a consultant mathematician with a good scientific argument."

"Will the mathematician testify?"

"She will be an excellent witness. I'll present the scientific argument first when the jury is fresh so that they can absorb it."

Phill nodded. "How are the Sodastroms?"

"They will make good witnesses. They look tragic. I'll put them on the stand late in the trial."

"How's your star witness, the psychic."

"He'll be great. Before I met him, I feared he might be a weirdo. He is a nice ordinary-looking, friendly guy. I'll arrange for him to do a demonstration.

"I'll rent a place up there and try to develop the idea that I'm a local."

There is another matter I need to discuss with you." He looked concerned. "Danae called me and voiced her concerns regarding the security situation. A man has been stalking you and might try to intimidate you and your witnesses."

"Yes, we discussed this during her last visit."

"There are new developments. Colson's security consultants have found that the person is on the FBI's radar. The suspect is a retired Army enlisted man trained as a bomb expert. He's linked to bombings in other states and is considered very dangerous.

"That scares me. This bomb specialist was seen around the trailer where I store my sailplane. He has was at an airport in Ogden studying how sailplanes are put together and possibly figuring out where he could hide a bomb. I'm not sure I want to fly before they catch this guy."

"Dave, Danae understands your concern. She said their security consultants would contact you and develop a plan to protect you and your sailplane."

"Good! I won't have time to fly it before the trial. Perhaps Colson's security people can find me an expert to inspect my bird after the trial."

"The bomb guy is a member of a group called Skeptemos. Danae gave me a link to their website. Have you seen it?"

"No,"

"Here, I'll put it on my computer screen."

The website opened with a montage of heroic medieval figures. Knights wearing white tunics with red crosses emblazoned on the front carried shields. Barbaric figures with firebrands marched in fierce groups. The montage ended with a heraldic crest with the same hieroglyph we had seen drawn on Candice's windshield and in the dirt near my sailplane trailer.

"Vince, This montage looks as though it was lifted from a Discovery Channel program or similar special on the Knights Templar."

A voiceover described how the group, Skeptemos, is carrying on the ancient tradition of fighting the forces of evil. Now, the agents of evil are those who would destroy pure science with the impure theories that promote superstition and fear.

That's scary.

"The good news is that even though their website makes them appear to be a large, organized group, the movement is only a few nuts," Phil responded. "We're not dealing with an al-Qaeda or ISIS here."

"Phil, I don't think I have time to hire bodyguards while I'm preparing for the trial."

"You can stick to your case. Colson has retained a high-end security firm to protect you and your witnesses. He hired a firm used to protect visiting heads of state. Colson once had a Pentagon job that brushed against the classified world. He has weighty concerns regarding industrial espionage. We can be confident his security consultants will be competent in their job."

Phil looked concerned. "Are you okay with this scenario?"

"If the security firm can keep the bombs out of my sailplane, I can live with it."

Phil looked relieved. "Good. I'll tell Danae of your concerns, and we'll continue with the case.

Back at my office, I texted Raven. "I'm back from the mountains. Dinner Saturday?"

An email message came from Candice saying she will have the draft of her new book by Friday. I replied that I'd be at UCLA Friday at noon and could stop by Cal State and get it.

Candice emailed back, "I'm going home at noon on Friday because I have a light day. Why don't you come by our house in the afternoon? You can meet Tom. He's very interested in what you're doing. He can tell you about the mental space-time travel he's done with his clients.'

I replied to her email. "I could be there around three or four o'clock, depending on the Friday afternoon traffic. Would you and Tom like to join me for dinner?"

"Yes. Great idea!"

Raven texted me a message: "Dinner on Saturday sounds great. Pick me up at 7:00? Let's go to Hernando's for margaritas."

I replied with a. ":-)"

She responded with ":-x"

11

CONVERGENCE

I was looking forward to dinner with Raven. She was to meet me downstairs to avoid me have to find a place to park. As I turned onto her street, she was crouched petting a neighbor's dog. She patted the dog on the head, gave it a small kiss on the forehead and turned toward me with a big smile. She opened the door and slid in. "Oh, I love Goldens. They're such loving dogs."

"You look beautiful. That shade of purple you are wearing is perfect for you."

She looked at me for a second, then brightened. "You're in a sparkling mood tonight. Full of Sierra sunshine or moon shine? Did you have a good week?"

"Rocky Butte was an interesting place, with fascinating people. I'll go up there next Wednesday and act like a local for a while before the trial starts. The trial won't last more than a week."

As we drove, I told her of Rocky Butte, the Judge, Agnes, and the gold pans. She listened with great interest.

After we sat and ordered margaritas and food, I told her of Steve and Georgia. "Steve is my main witness in the trial, the former CIA remote viewer who tried to help find the lost girl. He and his wife live in a mountain cabin, almost off the grid, at the end of unnamed dirt roads above Rocky Butte. They're a wonderful, loving couple, comfortable and affectionate with each other. Not the same as the uptight lawyers and wives I meet here in LA. Georgia has unusual psychic powers. When I was telling her about my home in the desert, she picked up pictures of you being there."

Raven smiled in a knowing way. "They sound great. You now act as though you're comfortable with these ideas of psychic powers. That's a great switch!"

"My vision of the freeway accident started a cascade of change in my thinking. The physics, the logic, the people, and my personal experiences flowed together. I now accept that these things happen. All of this stuff is within an expanded realm of science."

Raven's eyes sparkled with delight. "Although I don't understand this mathematical stuff, It's wonderful that you're experiencing these new understandings. Who would have believed! Wow! The energy level coming off your body is amazing."

She is looking at me with an expression I haven't seen before. What a wonderful energy.

"That's not the best part. I visited Dr. Candice Montgomery and her husband at their home in Altadena. Her husband, Tom Watson, a Hollywood-type composer/arranger, does personal counseling in something he calls space-time therapy.

"I asked him how it worked, and he said for me to try a simple memory procedure and see. My knee often hurts because I twisted it playing squash. I started by remembering a time when I had the sore knee. He had me follow that memory thread back to a childhood injury when I fell on my knee. Then, recollections of my knee hurting vanished. It hasn't hurt since then!"

"Not at all? That's amazing."

"Then, we did the same recalling procedure on an emotional thread that started the last time Zaza made me mad. That thread connected back to when I was mad at a friend in the second grade. Then, the emotional pain of being mad disappeared. Tom kept me recalling emotional threads on a variety of things."

"I'm amazed that you allowed yourself to do this. Go on!"

"After, two hours, a strange thing happened: I was doing recalls on incidents of me being mad at my brother. The thread connected back to my sixth birthday when we had a fight. Tom asked me if there was an earlier time, A vision came of someone who seemed like a brother—not my brother in this lifetime—standing next to an ancient biplane, the kind they flew in World War I. At that point, we had to stop because I had an incredible surge of happiness. I booked another session for tomorrow afternoon."

Raven looked startled. "Was that a past life? I have a friend who did past life therapy and claims she was all kinds of people, including Cleopatra. I've always had doubts about such claims. One time, my teacher friends and I were discussing who we might have been in past lives. Between us, we knew of four different people that said they had been Cleopatra."

"I have reservation about this whole idea. What are the physical means by which souls move from body to body when they change incarnations? The word population keeps growing. Where are the new souls coming from? Tom answers those questions. He says our recall of living in an another time is a psychic connection to another person in that past. No DNA or reincarnation is implied. It's a connection to a place in space-time that holds an idea, emotion, unfinished business, or physical injury. Tom said not to worry how or this connection exists."

She stared at me. "I've never seen you like this. Is there more? Your energy might blow me right out of this chair."

Our margaritas arrived.

"I've got to settle down. Tell me about your week."

Raven told me of her week of teaching and how she had a parent-teacher conference with a Beverly Hills Billionaire. We chatted while we ate, and I observed that the Mexican food was grounding.

"You're changing with this space-time stuff. I'd like to meet Candice and Tom sometime."

"I'm going there tomorrow. You could come along. Candice may not be there. Do you want to sit alone for two hours?"

"I'll take my Kindle to entertain myself. Could we stop by the Norton Simon Museum in Pasadena on the way home? It's time for another Impressionist fix. There are good places to eat in Old Pasadena, sidewalk cafes, and bistros. It's pleasant to wander around and shop this time of year. Have you ever been to the Norton Simon?"

"Not for a long time. It'll be a good way to ground myself after spending an hour or two traveling through space-time with Tom."

I took Raven's hand "One thing I like about you is how much space and time you can occupy. You can mentally go with me tomorrow, to Altadena, and then flash over to the museum, go through it, visualize the paintings, and then move through the list of sidewalk cafes, recalling the menus, and then go shopping, all in less than a minute."

Raven tilted her head down, glanced hesitantly at me and said, "You left out how I started the day" After a long theatrical pause, she said, "I was at my place, making breakfast for you."

That pleasant glow around my heart appeared. I raised my hand and said, "Waiter, check, please."

A late spring cold front had passed through Altadena during the night, carrying away the LA haze and smog, making the sky sparkling blue, and dotting the mountains with a procession of small puffy clouds.

I looked at the sky. "Today will not be much of a soaring day in the desert. This is a good day to be doing something else."

Like this! I love being with Raven.

Raven was admiring and commenting on the variety of architecture in the homes; Victorians from the early days of Altadena, old bungalows from the depression era, and Spanish style stucco. We agreed on what was ugly or beautiful. I was having fun.

We pulled up to Candice and Tom's house.

"Oh isn't that darling?"

We walked up to the front door. I saw a note taped to the glass. "Dave, I'm with another client. Go into the living room and make yourself at home. Coffee, tea, and a bowl of fruit are in the kitchen."

As we walked in, Raven exclaimed, "Oh, this is just perfect. Pasadena and this area have so many Craftsman homes. Notice the dark hammered copper light fixtures! Look at those green ceramic vases, the finely crafted bookcases, couch, rocking chairs. The fireplace of custom tiles. Oh, this is wonderful!"

"And," I added, "that painting is by a California Impressionist."

Raven walked to the picture, examined it and said, "This could be a Payne because it looks as if he painted the view from this back yard. Those mountains are the same. Payne liked to paint around here. See the detail in the wildflowers. While you are with Tom, I'll study this more."

I looked at her. *How did she get to be such an expert on California Impressionist paintings?*

Then, we heard Tom saying goodbye to his client, a well-dressed lady, at the front door. Tom came into the living room and greeted us with a hearty welcome."

After I had introduced Raven, she said, "I brought along plenty to read. I'll sit right here as quiet as a mouse."

I noticed that Tom looked at her with his far away gaze

He is sensing something psychic.

"Raven, I'm delighted you came along with Dave. He said you teach at Beverly High. You must meet many powerful and interesting parents."

"Yes, and kids wearing Rolex watches."

Ton looked at me. "I'd love to hear about it. But now I'd better get Dave in session. He is starting to go somewhere else in space-time. Make yourself at home and use the kitchen to make coffee or tea. There's a big bowl of fresh fruit. Sit on the back patio and enjoy the day. The bathroom is down the hall. We'll be two hours or so. A trail leaves the back yard and goes up the hill to a viewpoint. Watch out for snakes."

"Thanks, Dave told me about Mr. Spider. I think I'll visit him. I'll be careful not to disturb him."

"He's behind the avocado tree at the end of the yard."

Tom took me to his office.

Two hours and fifteen minutes later we emerged. I looked around and found Raven taking a nap on a chaise lounge in the shade on the back patio. As she heard the screen door open, she sat up.

She is beautiful!

"Back from space-time travels?"

"Yes. It was amazing."

"It looks like it. You're radiating that incredible energy!" Raven walked over and grabbed my arm and kissed me on the cheek.

Tom grinned.

I thanked him and then said our goodbyes. As we walked to the car, I said to Raven, "Will you drive? I'm still distracted, not totally back in the present."

"Still want to go to the Norton Simon?"

"Yes, that will be perfect. Let's have something simple for lunch?"

She thought a minute. "There's a latte and snack cart in the courtyard at the museum. They have sandwiches. How would that be?"

"Great." *It's wonderful she is here with me today.*

After we had driven away, Raven asked, "Do you want to talk about your session?"

"Yes, that's a good idea. I'm still trying to assimilate what I experienced in visiting that space-time.

"Tom took me back to the time I visited yesterday when my then brother was standing next to a biplane. It was at the start of World War I in Germany. My brother, died in a biplane crash. Tom made me stop, and I cried like a baby."

"You seem to be over it now."

"I got the grief out of my system. Then, we got into my flying in a German biplane squadron. The other pilots were a scary, brutal bunch of guys, fiercely and ruthlessly competing to be honored for shooting down the most enemy airplanes.

Raven looked at me wide-eyed. "I can sense your fear when you mention them. This is heavy."

I felt how the airplane flew and how it made turns and dives. The growl of the engine and the rattle of the machine guns were in my ears. There was confusing stuff I don't understand. There must be more of that story."

Raven closed her eyes. "I just got a mental picture from you. The airplanes were red and had black stripes on then."

I was shocked. *She's doing it again. I guess it's okay. How will I hold things back I don't want to share?*

Raven's eyes softened as she observed, "That all sounds like Dave Willard is himself becoming a psychic spy, peering into other space-times. Do you want to follow that with looking a Monet's Water Lilies?"

"Yes. I need grounding."

The Norton Simon Museum sits on Colorado, the main street of Pasadena, the path of the New Year's Day Rose Parade. As we walked up to the unassuming brown-tiled building, we passed several bigger-than-life Rodin bronze sculptures in a courtyard. We could see through the glass lobby into the garden. It had a food cart, large pond, hundreds of trees and shrubs, and many pieces of sculpture worked into the landscape. Two exhibition wings connected to the lobby.

We sat at one of the garden's wrought-iron tables, enjoying sandwiches. Raven said, "I love this place. We can sit and see works by these great sculptors. What a visual feast!"

She's full of surprises.

"I'm impressed by your knowledge of art. Do you teach Art and English?"

"No, my master's degree work included art history and art appreciation classes. Practice has taught me to view paintings at a deep level. With some artists' works, I sense the emotion of what the artist was experiencing as they painted the picture. One of my favorite landscapes, *Sous Bois*, by Cezanne, in the LA County Museum, shows a scene in the trees. After studying the work, I can smell the leaves, inhale the humidity, sense the love of the trees, and marvel at the shapes. It's as though I'm getting into Cezanne's head."

I laughed. "Now who is being a psychic spy?"

"I guess so. I've never thought it that way." She paused and then raised her finger. "Two years ago, I visited the Rothko Chapel in Houston that features his big panels, nearly black, painted shortly before he committed suicide. While studying his brooding canvases, a feeling of utter despair came over me, a sense of total failure. Even now, just thinking about that place makes me feel his anguish. Aargh! I've to keep my mind out of there." Raven shook her head back and forth as if she were shaking off water.

"You know, two months ago I'd have thought you were irrational talking of experiencing dead artist's emotions by looking at their paintings. Now, it seems reasonable."

Raven leaned over and squeezed my hand and then gave me an affectionate look I shall never forget.

What was that about?

She looked embarrassed. "Let's go into the galleries."

We spent an hour viewing the Impressionist and Post-Impressionist works by Manet, van Gogh, Matisse, Monet, etc. without saying much. I noticed that the vibration I sensed from her changed when she studied some of the paintings.

After a while, Raven put her palms to her eyes. "Let's walk in the garden: I'm getting visually saturated."

We walked into the garden. "Could that be one of the secrets of great art? A painting could be a ticket to travel in space-time to be with an artist."

Raven didn't respond. She gave me a version of the look she had given me at lunch.

High brown tile-surfaced walls of the same height and color as the museum surrounded the garden. In the center, there was a long pond covered with patches of water lilies and edged with rushes and reeds. A wide variety of trees, many in bloom, filled the garden and shaded a path that meandered around the pond. Bronze and granite statues rested near the water and under the trees, bathed in the soft ripple of reflected late afternoon sunlight.

We looked at each statue for a minute or more, sometimes walking over to read the nameplate and admire the surrounding plants or trees. A large dark metal nude woman, double life-sized, appeared to be tumbling sideways into the patch of lavender surrounding her base. Her arms stretched out in the air. Her feet flailed. Only her hip touched the base.

I hadn't noticed. We were holding hands

I walked over to the nameplate and read aloud, "Air."

Raven asked, "Aristide Maillol, right?"

I nodded yes.

"Raven, I feel like this woman when I'm around you. I'm about to tumble."

"Me, too," she answered smiling shyly, eyes looking downward. "Into a bed of lavender isn't all that bad."

I took her hand. "We should live together. I want to be around you as much as possible."

She turned and put her hands on my cheeks, gave me that look again, and smiled her mischievous smile. "I'd like that."

There was a long pause. Does she have second thoughts?

She gave me a long kiss. "Your place or mine?"

I was concerned. "Why the delay in answering?"

"Oh, I was at my apartment packing."

"Is this only until you go off to war in Rocky Butte next Wednesday?"

"No," I looked into her eyes, "I'm glad you're such a careful listener. This will be for much longer."

She cut me off. "I must warn you I'll redecorate your place, add more art works."

"No Rothkos, I hope."

She gave me a sly grin. "We'll see."

We started our togetherness at my apartment. Tomorrow was a legal holiday. I didn't want to go to my office, anyway. We stopped by Raven's apartment, and she packed up a few things. Then we stopped at a market. Raven wanted to cook a special dinner. I felt domestic and comfortable with the idea. We are a pair. I'm carrying bags of groceries of real food into my apartment, walking behind someone else who lives here.

Raven cooked a marvelous dinner. We ate by candlelight to the sound of romantic music. It was a great evening. I like the lavender.

The next morning, I awoke to the sound of Raven humming and wafts of breakfast and coffee filling the air. I lay in bed and reveled in my new domestic bliss.

We lolled and loved away the day, my best-ever holiday.

In the late afternoon, we sat on the couch in the living room still in our bathrobes. Raven leaned her back on me and worked with my iPad.

"I've been researching World War I flying. The German high command awarded a medal nicknamed the Blue Max to pilots who shot down lots of enemy aircraft. Here's a picture of famous German pilots. She handed me the iPad.

I looked, and my heart sink. Six aviators in overcoats wearing riding pants tucked into knee-high leather boots stand in a row. A seventh, the fiercest looking of the bunch, wears a double-breasted dress uniform. Wow!

Raven looked into my eyes. "I can sense your response. You really fear them."

"A strand of my 'web of life' is tied to that space-time. The pilot on the left of the picture wearing the dress uniform is a bitter enemy."

"He is wearing a medal around his neck." She studied the picture. "It's the Blue Max."

I pushed the iPad away. "He must have been the commander of the other men."

Raven scrolled a few pages on the iPad and then handed it back. "Here's a picture of one of their old airplanes."

I took the iPad. Adrenaline flowed. Fear. That must have been the type I flew.

My eyes closed. Wow! I am flying this airplane. It turns and climbs ease. The controls are stiff. The sound of the engine and smell of the exhaust fumes are familiar. Stick forward; it dives, the engine roars as it gains speed, starting a loop. Back hard on the stick. It climbs. The land horizon drops and clouds appear. My body squashes in my seat. The land horizon reappears upside down at the top of the loop. I stomp on the rudder pedal and yank back on the stick. The horizon rolls back to normal.

Raven grabs my hand. "What's going on? You're twitching. Open your eyes."

"Oh, I drifted into a time when I was flying one of those airplanes. It was so real and freaky. How could I fly an airplane I've never been in? Do maneuvers never learned in a sailplane? Look. I'm shaking and sweating."

"Well, you're back now. No, I'll change that. You are still on the front lines of the war. This is the bar where all the pilots gather to drink after missions, and I'm the hostess. Raven stood and posed as a waiter. Can I bring you a glass of wine, lieutenant?"

"Yes, I need it."

Raven disappeared and returned with two glasses of wine. As she handed me mine, her bathrobe fell open.

She whispered in a husky voice, "I have a thing for you brave men who fly those noisy machines. Can I do anything to take your mind off this terrible war?"

I walked into my office on Tuesday. I didn't even notice Carolyn doing her smile thing because I was feeling so good. When I got to my suite, Zaza wistfully sighed her "Good morning." She looked at me. "Okay, this looks like a dozen long-stemmed roses day. Flopsey, Mopsy, Cottontail or the bird Raven?"

"No flowers."

I saw a puzzled look on Zaza's face.

Carolyn called. "You have an unexpected visitor. He said his name is Mr. Burton. Do you know who he is?"

"No, can't say I do. Is he there now?"

"I'll check," Zaza buzzed Carolyn.

"He's there."

I walked into the lobby, and a tall man in a navy blue suit and dark aviator glasses rose out of a chair. "Mr. Willard?"

"Yes." He handed me his business card. It read, "A. Burton, Special Representative, EB Services."

I stared at it for a moment then recalled that EB Services was Colson's Security consultant firm, then nodded my head in recognition.

"Please let's go to my office."

This guy looks like an assassin.

"Let's take a walk?" he said in a stern voice.

I wonder if I get to come back.

"Okay." I then turned to Carolyn who was pretending to rearrange things on her desk. "Tell Zaza I've left for a while."

I followed Mr. Burton to the elevator. Not a word. He stood with his hands clasped in front of him staring at the door as we descended. I did the same.

I hope we're on the same side.

We exited. He didn't turn as he whispered in a low tone. "Let's go out into the plaza."

Our Century City building is on the edge of a park plaza shared with two other high-rises. It has a central fountain and benches under trees or next to landscaped plots for people to relax or have lunch. I followed Mr. Burton to an isolated bench. We sat.

"Please excuse the precautions. They are part of our business. As you know, the Colson Foundation retained us to provide security for you and your key witnesses from now until the end of the trial. I'm aware of Dr. Montgomery's scare at your parking garage, the discovery of surveillance devices on your car, the person seen around your equipment at CrystalSky Airport, and his visit to Rocky Butte, and Ogden. We know who he is. We have a plan for your security and the security of your witnesses at Rocky Butte.

"First, we will provide surveillance of your equipment at CrystalSky Airport. It sits in the open, and we want to park a vehicle in the vicinity to conceal a surveillance camera. Do you have any suggestions?"

I thought for a second. "I sometimes rent a jeep sedan from the tow pilot, Dan, to pull my sailplane trailer for off-road retrieves. Rent Dan's Jeep and park it near my trailer. It wouldn't seem out of the ordinary since a credible coat of dust covers it. You can trust Dan. Tell him you're doing it for me so I can catch whoever's been messing around with my trailer."

"We'll do that. Here are the arrangements for Rocky Butte.

"We've leased a dude ranch near there, which has a main house and six first-class cabins. You will stay in the main house with two of my people. Buster, one of my operatives, and his wife, Sofia, will be your bodyguards. They will also prepare the meals. They're experts at what they do.

Burton paused, and I interrupted. "Can I bring my significant other?" *I love saying that.*

Burton didn't flinch, but I thought he was mulling over the fact they hadn't found a significant other while checking me out.

"I need to go to Rocky Butte to mingle with people, so they'll consider me more like a local. The town grapevine is an asset I intend to use. It gave me the intelligence that there was someone checking up on me, the guy that was also spotted in Ogden."

"Yes, in answer to both requests. But your guest can't go into Rocky Butte during the trial. We don't want to risk a hostage situation. Whenever you go into town, a bodyguard will stay near you."

"That will be fine."

12

BUSTER

Wednesday I took the eight-twenty-five United flight from LAX to Sacramento. While waiting at the baggage carousel, I heard "Mr. Willard?" I turned around and saw a buff athletic-looking cowboy, five foot eleven, maybe thirty years old, wearing faded jeans, a battered Stetson, and scuffed cowboy boots worn down at the heels. His face was very tan and weathered, with wrinkles that made him look older than he was.

"I'm Buster Cabot. I'll get you to the ranch." He had a Texas cowboy accent.

He handed me his card that read "Buster Cabot, E.B. Services, Inc."

"Pleased to meet you."

Is this right? Shouldn't he be a uniformed driver instead of a cowboy?

As we watched, the bags circulate on the carousel, Buster volunteered that the ranch was an hour and a half from the airport. When my bags came, Buster helped with them and said, "Follow me," and continued out the terminal door. We walked to the first floor of the parking structure, identified as short-term parking. Buster walked over to a green pickup truck, a GMC from the 1960s with two large headlights, one on each front fender. It had rust everywhere eating through the faded green paint and making gaping holes in the bottom of the doors. Dirty wheels had long ago lost their hubcaps.

We loaded my bags into the truck bed alongside a toolbox and oily agricultural equipment.

This is called "First Class travel?

As I opened the door, it squeaked and then clanked as it closed. I was surprised that the interior gleamed in shiny black vinyl and polished chrome. Inside, the rusty truck was in mint condition.

We drove away on the airport road. Buster was quiet and concentrating on the rearview mirrors. When we came to the Exit-Return interchange, Buster took the Return branch, and we circulated through the service and car rental areas.

What's going on? Am I being kidnaped?

After we had departed the airport, Buster said, without the Texas cowboy accent, "Sorry for the delay, I wanted to make sure no one was following us. I should introduce myself. I'll be in charge of your security at the ranch and your personal bodyguard."

Is E.B. Services a low-budget operation?

Buster continued, "E.B. Services is my day job. It fills the time between my gigs as a stuntman."

"Like in the movies?"

"When I was in the Army Special Forces I had a lot of parachute experience. I started my stuntman career doing parachute jumps. Then, I branched out into Westerns, to play bad guys in fight scenes or fall off horses. I became a martial arts expert and was even in a Jackie Chan film. These days, I work in a harness supported by wires in acrobatic fight scenes, the kind where you run up walls and jump over buildings. This is a movie truck. It didn't get looking like this on its own. It's sometimes rented from me when I'm on a movie. It has a special suspension and a good engine."

He pressed on the accelerator pedal, and the tires spun, screeched and smoked.

"It handles well in chase scenes, with real bad guys or in the movies. It won't attract much attention in Rocky Butte."

I'm sure of that.

He reached underneath the center of the dash. Something clicked, and a compartment dropped open. In it was a gun but not a western revolver. It was a modern gun like I see in cop movies. Next to it was a small red cylinder shaped like a miniature fire extinguisher.

"Is that real?"

"Yes, and it's licensed and legal. That cylinder is bear spray. It's a harmless pepper spray that's designed to stop a grizzly bear at thirty feet. It's useful for protecting yourself when it is not necessary to shoot somebody, or you don't have the time to break some bones."

He seemed to take particular delight in saying, "break some bones."

"If you know the secret latches to pull, I'll show you later, the back of the seat folds down, and there are two shotguns and a bullet-proof vest there."

"Who are you protecting when you're not a lawyer's bodyguard in a small town?"

"E.B. Services has all kinds of clients. I've got another persona where I do the black suit with microphones up the sleeves kind of thing, drive armored limousines and talk with an English accent. We protect executives and entertainment people, rock stars, etc. Sometimes, it's an important person from a Middle Eastern country. For most of those jobs, we have a high profile and are visible walking with our clients or standing near the stage as they perform or give speeches. We make it apparent that there is a security detail protecting the client. We're trained by the same people that train the Presidential Secret Service.

"Mr. Burton, my boss at E.B. Services set different ground rules for you."

I hope so.

"Yes, I want to create the persona that I am 'a country lawyer from a small town like Rocky Butte' and not a 'big time city-slicker lawyer.' I asked Mr. Burton to arrange the security so that nobody in Rocky Butte, especially prospective jurors, would be aware of my protection."

"E.B. Services understands how to arrange covert protection. Danae at Colson often calls for covert protection when Dr. Colson is going somewhere dangerous to negotiate a business deal.

"Thanks. It is good to know you understand my concerns about appearing as a country lawyer. Tell me about the ranch and the arrangements."

"The Rocky Butte Adventure Ranch is ten miles south of town on a dirt road two miles from the highway. It has a main lodge where you will live and six plush cabins where visitors stay. We'll all eat family style in the main lodge. My wife, Sofia, and I will cook and serve as bodyguards. She's trained in martial arts and works as a stunt person in the movies."

I joked, "I'll be careful not to complain about the cooking."

Buster didn't flinch or laugh as he continued. "Your witnesses will fly to Sacramento as you did and then will be met by our representative. Our people will be wearing limo driver clothes and have Towne Cars. The witnesses will be driven to another airport to board a small twin-engine chartered plane that will fly them to the dirt strip on the ranch. I understand you'll have a guest."

"Yes, Raven Corbin. She'll come Saturday and stay for the length of our time here. My legal assistant, a young attorney, Elizabeth McKenzie, will join us. She'll ride with me when I drive to court."

Buster glanced at me. "We must insist that Raven stay on the ranch and out of Rocky Butte until the trial is over. We don't want to risk a hostage situation. Sofia will be her companion when she goes for a swim, hike, or ride."

"Will I have a car, or is this my transportation?"

I hope I didn't insult Buster.

Buster laughed. "No, we've prepared a respectable car for you. Nothing fancy, a Chevy Camaro two years old, suitable for a country lawyer."

"Prepared? Secret compartments with guns?"

"No, we've added a few security features that I'll show you later. We have photographs, background data, etcetera, on the guy who's stalking you. Our intelligence source says he's a member of a violent group, but he is now working alone. We have code named him 'Mr. S.' The good news is he doesn't have or use guns. He got sent up early in his criminal career for possessing a gun in a place he shouldn't have. Now he only likes explosives.

Oh! That's a relief.

"Who is your intelligence source?"

"The FBI and Homeland Security consider him of interest. I've briefed them on our security plans."

I'm glad to hear that.

"I have two of my guys in town staying at the Riverside Motel. You'll probably never meet them. They'll be doing things for me and might drive people to or from the courthouse. Danae has a lady with a San Jose Times press pass who will attend the court sessions. She'll keep Danae informed on what transpires. You'll receive a copy of her dispatches."

"Buster, I compliment you on your planning. It is very thorough. I won't have to worry about anything but the trial."

"Worrying is E.B. Services' job."

"By the way, what does the 'E.B.' in E.B. Services stand for?"

"*Executive Babysitting*, or so I've been told."

During the rest of the way to Rocky Butte, we talked about movies Buster had been in and a few of the interesting cases I had tried. When I mentioned the Norton Simon Museum, Buster discussed his favorite painting there, *The Rag Picker* by Manet. There was more to Buster than his cowboy persona.

After we had turned off the highway onto the dirt road, we drove for a half mile through the forest and then into a driveway that led to a clearing and a boxy two-story early 1900s farmhouse. It was gray, with white shutters, and a new roof. Four Sycamore trees, green with their late spring foliage, grew near it it.

"We've rented this old farmhouse. You'll let it be known around town that you're staying here. One of my guys, call him your stunt double, Cody Stevens, will stay here and provide a nice welcome for Mr. S. if he shows up.

"You should look around inside so you can talk as though you're familiar with the place. Inspect the kitchen so you can describe it to someone. It has been recently redone."

The couches and chairs in the living room looked new. I surmised that it was a vacation rental because the kitchen was complete with dishes and cooking utensils.

This looks like a nice place. Raven would like it

We got back in the truck and drove the mile and a half to the ranch.

The gateway had two posts and a lintel made of logs. The lintel across the driveway mounted three pairs of Texas Longhorn bull horns. A wrought iron sculpture on the top pictured a bucking horse ridden by a cowboy twirling a lariat.

The ranch brand, a large letter R with a bar underneath, hung by chains.

The road from the gate wound downhill past a meadow filled with spring wildflowers to a slight rise and the ranch house. It was a large factory-made log house, two stories high with two dormer windows protruding from the roof that extended over a large, covered porch. Four rocking chairs sat on the porch.

As we pulled up in front, I saw a woman sitting in one of the rocking chairs. She got up and came out to greet us. She kissed Buster and then turned to me with a hand turned out to introduce herself.

"Hi, I'm Sofia. You must be Dave Willard. We're here to make sure you have a safe and enjoyable stay."

She had a strong handshake. Sofia wore a plain blue denim dress, with a heavy silver and turquoise necklace, and a variety of matching silver bracelets. Long, black braided hair fell the length of her back. A dark complexion and brown eyes made her appear to be a Native American.

Buster laughed. "I haven't seen you in that get-up since we left Taos! It looks good." He turned. "We were back there on a Western shoot. Although Sofia is of Portuguese descent, she gets cast in Indian roles. She is in her reservation diva costume. Wrong tribe for Rocky Butte though."

"I think it's cute," replied Sofia.

"Here, Dave, I'll show you around. This is the main lodge. There are six cabins nestled in the woods, three on the other side of the meadow and three behind the house. Down below there, in the back, are caretakers, maids, and hands' quarters, plus a barn with five horses in the corral. Two maids, who speak little English, and a wrangler, Ben, are the only people there now. We gave everyone else a vacation to make sure nobody went to town and talked about our operation. If you or your guests want to go riding, see Ben. He has a Jeep for rides to and from the airstrip or to the lake where there's a swimming beach, six rowboats, a canoe, and picnic spots. Except for your friend Raven, people need not be escorted anywhere on the ranch.

We then went over to a dilapidated-looking pickup with a camper shell on the back, parked near the lodge. Buster walked around and opened the camper shell door. There was no roof. A satellite dish filled the space.

"This provides secure high-speed internet service for any research you might need to do during the trial. We're too far out in the boonies for cable or DSL. The rig has a miniature cell site so you and your guests can use their phones. The lodge has a satellite TV."

We went into the lodge. The log walls gleamed with varnish. The chairs and sofa were made of aspen or birch-wood and had inviting deep brown leather cushions. Rugs woven in a Native Southwestern American style covered the floors and walls. A large river rock fireplace filled one end of the room.

Very Western. Raven will be pleased there are no mounted animal head trophies.

Buster showed me a bedroom off the kitchen. "This is where Sofia and I'll sleep, handy to respond to any need."

"You and your guest will stay in the suite upstairs. There's an office with a small conference table. We put your boxes picked up by the courier there. The satellite rig in the camper provides Wi-Fi so you and your guests can have internet access anywhere in the house."

Sofia invited us to follow her to the porch for lunch, carrying a platter of sandwiches. "I have iced tea," she said. "But there's beer in the fridge. Use the kitchen to get anything you want day or night. Make yourself at home."

"Thanks. By the way where's the car I'll drive?"

"Cody is bringing it up tomorrow."

After lunch, I excused myself to rest and get settled in.

Sofia said, "Dinner at six, happy hour at five."

The sun burst through my bedroom window. I saw a sparkling Sierra morning.

Downstairs, Sofia was alone in the kitchen, holding a mug of coffee, sitting in a chair with her legs pulled up under her bathrobe.

"It's cold. Pour yourself a coffee while I make breakfast."

I poured a cup of coffee. "Don't bother with breakfast now; I'm going for a run. How far is the lake?"

"A mile. Go past the stables and turn right at the fork in the trail." She walked to the cupboard and took out a canister of bear spray tucked in a small holster on a belt. "Here, take this with you. It's good for lots of things."

"Is there a bear problem?"

"No, but you never know what you might run into. Rumors about Sasquatch."

"He can be a bad one." I didn't protest. There were mountain lions in the area. What else is there to fear in these woods?

It was a pleasant run to the lake on a carpet of dry needles. I stopped to rest–the pine-scented air was thin at this altitude–and enjoy the view of the sparkling lake and the surrounding forest. I sat down on a soft bed of needles underneath a tree, shifted my weight to remove a small cone while listening to a scolding jay. The sun felt warm on my face as my eyes closed. The sound of a single-engine airplane two-thousand feet up intruded. It flew away to the east. The engine noise faded. I relaxed. My mind drifted. My eyes blurred, and I dropped into a meditative state.

Then, a movie began in my minds' eye. A dozen biplanes circled, dog-fighting, killing. The sounds of machine guns firing, engines revving filled the air as planes climbed, turned, and dove. Black smoke streamed as planes spun and plummeted.

I was flying a biplane and pursuing another airplane laboring along below me. It was an observation plane, one with a pilot and a machine gunner. It didn't maneuver to evade me.

One pass with my machine guns blaring caused the pilot and gunner to slump down. Smoke poured from the engine. I circled to make sure it crashed. The machine gunner stood up with blood pouring from his wounds. His machine gun jammed. He pounded on it. As my biplane grew near, I saw that the gunner was a mere boy, a teen with terror in his face. My hand came off my machine gun trigger. He was an innocent-looking boy. As my wingtip passed by the plane, I saw the pilot's head slumped over the side of the cockpit. He too was a mere teen. Not old enough to shave. Judging by his flying skills, he had only learned to take off and land before being sent out on a reconnaissance mission.

This air war is against children!

The plane crash in flames. Dogfights were supposed to be between chivalrous knights of the sky. We shouldn't be be sent out to murder children.

I decided "No more 'combat' missions for me."

The vision returned after a short nap. Military personnel assembled on a parade ground. The commandant tore the buttons and insignia patches from my uniform. I was disgraced, cashiered.

My eyes opened full of tears. I walked to the ranch house, trying to make sense of my vision.

Why is this vision coming now, a hundred years later?

In the kitchen, Sofia glanced at me, then looked carefully. "You okay? Did you run into Sasquatch?"

"I'm okay. I recalled the memory a terrible time in that my hometown, the discovery of a body in the woods."

That had happened; it was a passable explanation.

"Go into the dining room. I'll bring you breakfast there. Buster is there with Cody."

Buster introduced me to Cody who didn't look like a western movie stuntman. He was my height and weight, with brown eyes, and a short haircut made to appear spiky.

He's a mirror image of me!

Buster explained. "Cody is your stunt double who will be living in the 1900s farmhouse. He is well trained, as are all members of our organization, and will give Mr. S. an appropriate welcome if he shows up."

I looked in astonishment at Cody and said, "Are we related? You look like my brother."

We walked outside to the black Camaro parked next to Buster's truck. Buster handed me the keys. "We've modified the alarm system. Our sources say Mr. S. likes to rig car bombs. You have a special electronic door opener on the key chain. It has two indicator lights. If either of those is lit, don't go near the car. The yellow light indicates that someone has been in the car since you locked the door. The red light shows that someone has had the hood open. If either of those lights is on, walk away. I'll always be nearby to take care of you. This is a very important instruction. Also, don't give your car to anyone else to drive unless it's at my instruction."

"I understand. Can I use it to go into town for dinner tonight at Bob's Cafe?"

"Yes, I'll follow you in my truck. You plant the idea that you're staying at the decoy farmhouse and pick up anything from the town gossips. Get the townspeople used to this Camaro being your humble car."

Back in the lodge, Sofia handed me a hanger with a white Hawaiian shirt having hula girls on the front and back.

This is ugly.

"Wear this into town. It may not be your usual style, but we want you to stand out. It's part of the plan."

That evening I drove to have dinner with Agnes at Bob's Cafe and parked the Camaro in front of the cafe. There were eight people in the cafe. Four men in Stetsons sitting at one booth looked at the Camaro. Three women, maybe belonging to the men, sat in another booth busily talking. A man wearing a Caterpillar Tractor ball cap occupied a booth at the end of the restaurant. The ladies bent over in whispered conversation, perhaps speculating about me.

I sat on the same stool at the counter that I sat on during my first visit. Agnes walked over and announced, "The dinner special is pork chops, best in the county."

"I can't pass that up. I'll have an MGD."

Agnes announced, "One Miller Genuine Draft coming up." She slid the order slip onto the carousel at the service counter and brought me my beer. "I didn't expect you until next week when the trial starts."

Buster drove up in his green pickup.

"I came up to do a little relaxing before the trial. I've rented a place ten miles down the hill, off on a dirt road. It was a farmhouse and is now a vacation rental."

Agnes thought a minute and then said, "Is it a boxy gray house with white shutters?"

"Yes'."

Buster came in and sat at a booth, without either of us acknowledging each other.

"That's the old Williams' house. They used to own several ranches around here. I heard they fixed it up."

"You're right. It has a fine new kitchen, it looks recently repainted, and has new furniture."

The ladies were huddling again.

Cook rang the bell, and Agnes retreated to deliver orders.

After the bell rang again, Agnes brought my special.

"Looks good."

"Best in the county. You staying there alone?"

I nodded yes as I took my first bite. Agnes walked away.

She also served Buster the special.

After I finished, Agnes asked. "Get you anything else?"

"No, thank you. that was quite filling." Buster left and was sitting in his pickup, using a toothpick. He looked deep in thought. I left Agnes a generous tip under my plate and walked to the cash register to pay my check. Agnes gave me my change.

"Come see us again soon."

I drove back toward the ranch. Buster was a good distance behind me. I turned onto the dirt road, and Buster passed me and stopped by the driveway to the old Williams house. I stopped behind him. Cody came out from behind a tree and walked to my car. He wore the same hula shirt I was wearing.

"You can ride with Buster the rest of the way."

I stood and watched Cody drive my car into the driveway before I joined Buster.

"This will be the routine," said Buster.

"What is he going to do to pass the time? Sit and watch television or read?"

"Cody is a screenwriter. Two of his scripts are now movies. He's working on the rewrite of a script he sold that will be going into production this summer. If someone peeks into the window of the farmhouse, they will see a man hard at work on his laptop, looking ever so much like a lawyer preparing a case. He even has a bunch of law books scattered around."

As we drove to the ranch, we exchanged views on the best pork chops in the county and other worldly matters.

Friday was spent getting ready for the trial. In the courthouse, I filed papers and then strode to Bob's Cafe for lunch. Buster drove by but did not stop. Agnes said the special was one of the cook's favorites, an open-faced chili hamburger.

One can't get this food on Melrose Avenue. I'll bring Raven here for a treat and celebration after we win the case.

When I drove to the ranch, Buster followed. After the switch with Cody at the Williams' place, I asked Buster where he had eaten lunch.

"I had fine dining at the Tasty Freeze."

Back at the ranch, I decided to enjoy the evening and take a nap in the hammock behind the lodge. I was dozing off, enjoying the late afternoon sun reflecting off the needles of the pine trees, listening to the wind and raucous stellar jays.

My mind drifted into a meditative state. Suddenly, I was back in my biplane time. I was standing in my desecrated uniform, talking to a woman dressed in a white lace dress and wearing a wide floppy lace brimmed hat. She was angry, scolding me, and shaking her finger. I sensed I was sad and betrayed! She stormed away. My heart sank. The pictures faded. I felt a profound despair.

Sleep returned. I woke up at as the sun set. The bad feelings were gone. *A great burden has lifted! A new sense of freedom!* A joyful mood came over me.

I sat up, put my feet on the ground and took out my cell phone. Tom answered right away. He was composing but didn't mind the interruption.

I described my visions, the dogfight ending in my disgrace, and the rejection by the lady in white.

Tom said firmly, "I thought I told you not to try this at home. You can get screwed up with your attention stuck in another space-time. Go over the last part of each vision slowly."

He listened.

"You're okay. I'm sensing your vibration from here; I can tell you have dealt with whatever that was. It's okay to analyze what it means, but don't go back there again. If you sense you're drifting into that meditative state, think of something else. Promise me this?"

"Agreed. what do I need to watch out for right now?"

"If you start to drift, grab onto or feel some objects around you. That will help ground you. When can you come in again?"

"I might be up here a couple more weeks."

"Be careful. Is Raven up there with you?"

"She'll be here tomorrow."

"Good. Tell her to punch you or slap you if you drift down into a meditative state. Better yet, tell her to kick you in the balls. That will ground you. Nobody travels in space-time bent over in pain. Let's get together as soon as you get back to LA. Call me again if you get in trouble."

"Thanks. Goodbye."

I walked around picking up and examining pinecones and feeling and closely examining the bark of the trees until I felt confident my attention was in the present.

I walked to the lodge. Buster lounged in one of the easy chairs, listening to music.

He sat up and fumbled with his iPhone. "What's happening?" He stared at me with a puzzled expression. "You look like a cat that has just eaten a double order of canaries."

"Oh. I was snoozing in the hammock and had an interesting dream."

"She arrives tomorrow doesn't she?"

"Yes, but the dream wasn't of her. I dreamed of flying biplanes in World War I."

"Is that a good thing?"

"Yes. I am learning about myself; why I spend time in the desert flying a sailplane and trying to complete flying goals that will win me an award."

Buster looked puzzled. "What's the award?"

"The award is a half-inch wide diamond encrusted badge I can wear on my hat when I go soaring."

Buster picked up his iPhone, put his earbuds back in. "Whatever."

He is right. Diamond badge? I don't need it now. Indeed. Whatever!

13

TOGETHER AGAIN

It was hard for me to concentrate on work the next day. I was excited, anticipant. Raven's plane was coming in at two-thirty. We had only lived together for two joyful days, and it felt as though we had always been together. These four days of separation seemed like an eon.

I rode to the dirt airstrip with Ben in the Jeep. He was an authentic silent cowboy type; slim but muscular, six-feet-two, around thirty years old, with chiseled features.

The bright Sierra sun blazed. I moved over into the shade and headed Tom's warning not to drift off in space-time. After a few minutes of my enjoying the quiet, the distant sound of a twin-engine airplane interrupted my reverie.

The plane circled low over the field as the pilot checked the windsock. Excitement at seeing Raven increased. The airplane disappeared and then a long minute later appeared at the end of the runway. It made a smooth landing and taxied. The engines sputtered to silence. Raven was sitting in the back seat and Elizabeth McKenzie, my jury assistant, sat in the front.

Elizabeth climbed out first, dressed in a business suit. I shook her hand. "Welcome." Raven jumped down and ran to me and gave me a big kiss. I feel whole again.

Elizabeth, six-foot-two woman, with a low maintenance, short haircut had been a member of the U.S. Olympic volleyball team. She had great powers of observation that made her a valuable trial assistant. Her volleyball training allowed her to sense everything going on between everyone in a room. She has a useful ability to read juries.

"Raven, the Lodge is about a mile away. I see you're wearing tennis shoes. Want to walk?"

"Sure."

Elizabeth was eyeing Ben as he loaded the baggage. She appeared interested by the fill of his Levis.

"Ben, we'll walk. Elizabeth is staying in cabin two. Show her around the lodge and then take her to her cabin. We'll be there later."

Raven squeezed my hand. "I missed you. It feels like we've been apart for months." We hugged.

As we walked holding hands, Raven told me of the frantic activity in ending the school year. I told her of the fine dining in Rocky Butte, how Buster and Sofia were our bodyguards. She displayed mock disappointment when I told her she wouldn't be able to enjoy the fashionable eating establishments in Rocky Butte until after the trial. Then, we can have a night on the town including dining and clubbing at the Claim

Jumper and Diggings if we could talk Buster and Sofia into going with us.

"I've had more interesting new visions. The biplane thing came again, this time in more detail. I was a Word War I German fighter pilot. Early in the war dogfights were chivalrous combat, a modern version of noble medieval knights jousting in armor. Later, as the allies put more planes in the air, it turned into a wholesale slaughter of untrained pilots. In a vision, I saw the faces of two flyers in an airplane I shot down. They were mere boys, English teenagers. I refused to fly again to kill innocent children. They court-martialed me and publicly tore the insignias and rank from my uniform."

"That must have hurt." Raven looked concerned. "How could they have expected you to kill children?"

"In another vision, I saw a woman scolding me for disgracing her. I felt abandoned. Maybe that's where my trust issues originated.

"My passion for flying sailplanes must derive from those World War I times. I don't think I've lost my interest in flying, but it'll be different, less serious, and more fun."

"Wow! You're getting a lot out of this space-time travel. Have you talked to Tom about all of this?"

"Yes, I did. He told me to be careful and not to do it alone, unguided. It's possible to get mentally stuck in another time. You can help me stay in the present. If I start to drift in space-time, you should do something to get me grounded, such as take me to bed and jump on me."

She chuckled and then added with a wry smile, "Oh, the sacrifices one must make for mental health."

We walked arm-in-arm. I relish having her near.

Buster and Sofia greeted us. Sofia looked delighted to meet Raven. "It'll be good to have another woman around to share girl-talk. Here, let me show you the lodge."

Buster and I talked for a while, and he related that his men in town had picked up the gossip: a lawyer had moved to town and was buying the old Williams' place.

I laughed. "The subterfuge is working."

He commented that Elizabeth looked athletic. She had asked him which trails to use for a five-mile run.

Sofia and Raven returned from the kitchen. "Raven has given me ideas for dinner. Buster and I need to go to town to get groceries. We'll be back in a couple of hours."

"Stay near the lodge. One of my men is watching from that pickup parked by the driveway. While you are inside, keep the doors locked." We walked out on the porch and watched them drive away. We waved at the pickup, and it flashed its lights. Raven looked at me and said, "Emergency! He is drifting out of the present. Must take immediate action."

14

EVIL PLAN

Unknown to Dave, somebody was using this night to visit CrystalSky Airport and tamper with Dave's sailplane. He. drove his white van, lights off, in the light of the quarter moon, to the sailplane trailer.

I will destroy this agent of the forces of evil, one of those who would move the world back into superstition and fear by promulgating false beliefs in the name of a false science. The attorney will die a deserved, terrible death.

He chuckled to himself.

The Skeptemos Order will honor me for this feat. I can see the ceremony. The members in their white hooded robes, emblazoned with the red flame crosses, will chant and place a wreath of laurels on his head.

He. parked his van near the sailplane trailer, went into the back and pulled the black curtains over the windows. By a dim light, he assembled his bombs.

I'll use this flare that burns making poisonous smoke and kills gophers. How fitting for a lawyer to die like a varmint. I set the detonator to go off after the sailplane gets two thousand feet above the airport.

He gave the bomb a little kiss. *I'll make this second bomb a half stick of dynamited have it go off two minutes after the smoke bomb. He held the dynamic to his cheek. I love you little bomb. Make me happy and do your work.*

After turning off the light, he theatrically tip toed to the sailplane trailer cradling the bombs in his arms over his heart. An outside nightlight on a nearby hangar provided him with enough illumination to do his work. He put on latex gloves and used the key made from a wax impression to unlock the trailer. He had planned his procedure while watching the pilot rig the sailplane in Ogden, The bombs were placed behind and under the pilot's seat. He removed the parachute, turned it over and placed a locking pin in the ripcord to prevent it from working. He put everything back and then closed and locked the trailer and returned to his van.

As he drove away, he laughed to himself at the cleverness of his plan. *I can see it now. The attorney is behind the tow plane. At two thousand feet the smoke bomb goes off filling the cockpit with black, poisonous smoke. He struggles to open the canopy before he is overcome. He tries to fly the sailplane back to the field and then the second bomb under his seat goes off. Kaboom!*

Or maybe he decides to bail out after the smoke bomb goes off. He jumps and pulls the ripcord. Nothing happens! The attorney falls in terror to his death.

Ha, ha, ha. ha. I want to be there to watch this creation.

15

THE JURY

Monday morning, Buster drove Elizabeth and me to the Williams' house where we picked up our car to drive to court. Buster asked for a five-minute lead and drove off in his pickup.

Elizabeth briefed me on what she had discovered searching the internet. "Sheriff Bogend's father was a Bible-thumping Southern evangelical preacher. If we probe that, we might expose irrationality, strong beliefs in the Devil, and fundamentalist ideas. It would be great if we could get him to launch into a Bible-thumping tirade."

I think I can bait him. I'll put on my "from a logging town country boy" act.

Elizabeth looked around when she first saw downtown Rocky Butte. "Toto, I have a feeling we're not in Kansas, anymore."

I pointed out the nightlife spots and opportunities for fine dining.

Elizabeth shook her head. "I'd say this is about as far from the end of Melrose that one can get."

We parked in the courthouse parking lot. I noticed Buster and another rough-looking character sitting in his pickup.

Ever vigilant. I like that.

As we walked up the empty steps of the courthouse, Elizabeth admired the building. "Stick with Dave Willard, and you can end up in the big time! Imagine, getting to trial before eight. You go ahead. I'll handle the reporters."

The courtroom hadn't changed since it was construction in 1922. Waist-high, dark wood wainscoting accented beige walls that led to a ceiling of pressed tin squares. Two windows and four hanging shaded fixtures provided the light. The spectator's area sat about a hundred. American and California flags flanked the usual jury box, tables, and judge's bench. A witness box and court reporter's desk sat under a portrait of George Washington and the County Seal.

The Bailiff was talking to the jury pool seated in the last few rows of the spectator area. He outlined how the trial would be conducted, when there would be breaks and recess for lunch, parking arrangements, use of cell phones, and other administrative procedures.

I greeted the Sodastroms at our table and introduced Elizabeth. Ann and Ed Sodastrom looked tired and sad.

"I regret having to put you through this again. It should be over in a few days. Let Elizabeth or me know if there is anything I can do to make you more comfortable."

They look tragic. I am sorry for that, but it's just what I need.

Then, we introduced ourselves to Dean Buttress, the County Counsel who was there alone. His suit was rumpled, and his shoes scuffed. He had a dull look in his eyes and seemed tired.

Elizabeth whispered as we sat down, "Dean Buttress looks like an attorney who has been at it too long and lost too many. I think I smelled alcohol on his breath. He might have drunk his breakfast. The District Attorney must have assigned him because his office thinks that this case has no merit."

I whispered back, "I Agree. Or maybe they want to get rid of him."

I wonder if Stevens and Bracken is trying to get rid of me by putting me on this case. Am I the pot calling the kettle black?

The bailiff finished talking to the jury pool, moved everyone to the first rows of the spectators' seating, and disappeared through a door behind the judge's bench. In a minute he returned and said, "All rise. Department Three of the Superior Court of Rocky Butte is now in session. Judge Jeremiah Cartwright presiding."

The Judge walked to behind the bench and shouted, "Please be seated."

"Good morning, ladies and gentlemen. Calling the case of the Edward and Ann Sodastrom versus The County of Rocky Butte and Sheriff Alfred Bogend. Are both sides ready?"

Plaintiff?"

"Yes, your honor. David Willard and Elizabeth McKenzie representing the Sodastroms are ready."

"Defense?"

Dean Buttress looked surprised.

He rose and said, "Yes your honor. The defense is ready."

The judge frowned while looking at Buttress and said, "Very well. Bailiff, select the first panel to be seated."

The bailiff called fourteen juror numbers. Twelve sat in the jury box and two sat in the alternates chairs.

Judge Cartwright then said, "I have questions to ask every prospective juror. Other members in the jury pool are to make a note of the number of every question that you might have answered 'yes.' I will not repeat the questions every time a new prospective juror is selected.

"Question number 1: Raise your hand if any members of your family or extended family are law enforcement officers?"

No hands were raised

"Question number 2: Does anyone have a medical reason or personal hardship that would make it difficult to serve as a juror in this case?"

(No hands.)

"Question 3. Does anyone know or has dealt with the Sodastroms, Sheriff Bogend, or their attorneys?"

Six hands went up and were dismissed; four were personal friends of the Soddastroms, one was Sheriff's brother-in-law, and one had been falsely arrested by the Sheriff.

The Judge then continued with twenty more general questions. Two jurors were dismissed for having "yes" answers and replaced from the jury pool. They were questioned and then replaced until all juror seats were filled.

The judge asked the final twelve jurors to state their name, occupation. spouses occupation, and residence

When the judge had finished his questions, he turned and said, "Plaintiff. Your turn."

I stood up. "I come from a small town like this in Northern California, and everyone knew everyone and their business. Has anyone tentatively made up their mind about this case?"

(No hands)

"Has anyone discussed this case at length with someone?"

A woman raised her hand.

I checked the iPad that Elizabeth had prepared showing the position of each juror in the box and their name and occupation and other notes.

"Ms. Wells, who have you discussed this case with?"

She sat up straight and looked around nervously. "My minister."

"What was the gist of this conversation?"

"It must have been God's will if she died," she said with a determined tone.

Just what I need on the jury

"Thank you, Ms. Wells."

I looked at each face of the rest of the jurors. "Please raise your hand if you share this view?"

None raised their hands. Elizabeth was taking notes on how others responded to the question.

"Have any of you consult with a professional psychic?"

No hands went up. *Good!*

"Do any of you have friends or family members who have consulted with a psychic?"

No hands. *Not surprising because this county has a conservative voting record.*

"Anyone gone to a fortune teller?"

Elizabeth handed me a note, "Check Mr. Garth, juror 7. He didn't like those questions."

"Mr. Garth. *This guy looks bored.* You said you are a high school teacher. What subjects do you teach?"

"I teach science and mathematics."

"What journals or scientific magazines do you subscribe to?"

"Scientific American."

"That's a good magazine. Do you visit scientific websites?"

"Yes."

"Thank you, Mr. Garth."

I don't need him on a jury trying to convince everyone else that there is no scientific evidence that ESP exists.

"Does anyone else read science or mathematics magazines?"

I looked at my iPad for the name of the frightened-looking man who had raised his hand.

This one is a guy that worries about doing the right thing.

"Mr. Tinder, I understand you are a retired geologist. What science or mathematics magazines do you read ?"

"The Oil and Gas Journal."

"Do you think opinions expressed in that magazine could influence your ability to be impartial in this case?"

"No."

"Thank you, Mr. Tinder."

Elizabeth slipped me a note that said, "Enough science."

I looked at my iPad and checked the name of a woman in the second row who looked eager.

"Ms. Winters. Do you understand that in a criminal case the jury must convict if the evidence shows, 'beyond a reasonable doubt,' that the accused is guilty?"

"Yes, that's what they always say in movies on TV."

"Do you understand that this is a civil case with different rules?"

"No, I guess I don't know the difference."

"One big difference is what the law calls the burden of proof. In the small town I grew up in, people had a habit of showing you something instead of telling you. Look at the Rocky Butte County seal on the wall. Do you see the blindfolded lady holding a balance scale in her hand?"

"Yes."

"She signifies justice and is weighing the evidence with the scale. You see that one side of the scale is only slightly higher than the other?"

"Yes?"

"Do you understand 'negligence' is proven by the "preponderance of the evidence?" I put my right hand to slightly below my waist and lowered my left hand to slightly above my belt. "The county seal seems to be showing a situation where the scale is only slightly tipped. Do you think this illustrates the idea of the 'preponderance of evidence'?"

"Yes."

"Do you understand that if this were a criminal case, like someone stealing a car, the burden of proof would have to be 'beyond a reasonable doubt?'" I held my left up at neck height and my right palm up at waist height. "The evidence of 'guilty,' shown by my right hand at my waist, must greatly overweigh the evidence of 'not guilty.'"

Ms. Winters nodded yes.

"Do you understand the difference between 'beyond a reasonable doubt" and "preponderance of the evidence'?" I showed the difference by moving my hands as I spoke

Ms. Winters smiled and said, "Yes."

"Thank you." I smiled at her, and she gave me a big smile back.

She is okay. Nice and compliant.

"Mr. Segar. "Do you understand the difference between 'beyond a reasonable doubt' and 'preponderance of the evidence?'"

He sat up straight and spoke with authority. "Yes."

A good disciplined thinker.

Other jurors were nodding their heads in agreement.

"Mr. Segar, you stated that you are a retired building planner. Is that correct?"

"Yes."

"Were you employed by Rocky Butte County?".

"No. I was a planner in the Building Department of Three Peaks County."

Good a nice rule-based thinker.

"Did your duties there require dealing with Three Peaks or Rocky Butte county law enforcement agencies?"

"No. I was never involved with code enforcement."

"Do you think your experiences as a employee of Three Peaks County could influence your ability to be impartial in this case?"

"No."

I think he will be a good juror because he knows how county governments work.

Elizabeth handed me a paper that read, "Keep this one. dismiss these jurors . . . ."

"Your Honor, I move to dismiss jurors numbers 5,2,1. and 6."

The Judge looked at his watch. "Those jurors are dismissed. It is now one-forty-five. We will recess for one hour for lunch."

I looked around the courtroom and saw Buster in the back row and his associate sitting in a different row.

Good. Ever vigilant! He looks like he has either put on weight or is wearing a bullet proof vest.

Elizabeth and I retired to a conference room with our sack lunches. "Really the big-time." Elizabeth unwrapped her sandwich and opened her canned drink. "Other courts give you an hour and a half for lunch."

"In my pretrial meeting with the judge, he said we would have long court days and a short trial. People have business to run and a tourist trade to serve.

"I think the selection went well, thanks to you, Elizabeth."

"I hope Buttress doesn't dismiss the building planner. This is a good jury. We got rid of the 'God's will' woman and the two men who seemed to agree as she answered your question, the science guy, and the guy who looked angry. The county planner will understand rules and policies. There aren't any wild cards in there. The two older ladies, number 7 and 8, sneered at Buttress when he acted hung-over by snoozing and stumbling around. Maybe they think he is an alcoholic."

"Thanks for your expert observation and help with that, Elizabeth."

"Yes, we can accept this jury if the replacements are okay."

The judge reconvened the court at two-forty-five and replaced the four dismissed jurors.

I questioned them briefly and then said, "Your Honor, The Plaintiff accepts the jury."

Judge Cartwright looked at Dean Buttress who was staring blankly out of the window and said. "The defense may examine the Jury."

Buttress stood up slowly and thumbed through papers on the table without seeming to find what he was looking for. He looked at the jury. "Mr. Stratton, was you brother-in-law arrested by Sheriff Bogend for stealing a car and sent to jail for six months?"

Mr. Stratton said "Yes."

"Your Honor, move to dismiss."

Buttress' speech is kind of slurred. He must have drunk his lunch.

The judge replaced the juror.

Buttress said, "The defense accepts the jury."

Judge Cartwright looked at me, and I said. "The plaintiff accepts the jury."

I got to keep the county planner!

While the Bailiff swore the jurors and the Judge gave them instructions on not discussing the case with others, reading papers or watching TV News, I talked with Elizabeth.

She whispered in my ear, "A woman in the spectator area looks like a reporter. It must be the San Jose Times person who Danae hired to send trial summaries."

"Yes, I see her."

The judge adjusted his chair and rearranged papers on his desk.

"I will now hear opening statements. Mr. Wellard"

"Your Honor, ladies, and gentlemen of the jury:

My name is David Wellard. My associate Elizabeth McKenzie and I represent Ann and Ed Sodastrom in their negligence case against Sheriff Bogend and the County of Rocky Butte concerning the death of their daughter Lucy. We will show Sheriff Bogend was solely in command of the search and rescue operation undertaken to find Lucy. You must find that Sheriff Bogend was negligent in not acting as any reasonable person would and ignored two significant clues as to

Lucy's location. He also did not employ all the resources available to him. Thank you."

The Judge looked at the defense counsel and said, "Would the defense like to make an opening statement?"

"Yes, your Honor."

He bumbled around on his desk for his notes. "We all go to the movies and watch TV. Popular series have mediums and psychics solving complicated criminal cases. Those stories come from screenwriters. On the screen, Superman can fly; Spiderman can swing through Manhattan on threads of webs; medieval Merlins can conjure Dragons, and psychics identify killers.

"You can rely on your experience to judge what is fact and what is fiction.

"The essence of this case is whether Sheriff Bogend should have listened to a stranger, claiming to be a psychic, and diverted his valuable search and rescue resources down Bear Creek, thereby lessening his search in Sheffield Valley where tracks showed Lucy had gone. Sheriff Bogend acted as a reasonable person would and ignored a stranger who claimed to have a magical power to know where Lucy was. You must find that Sheriff Bogend was not negligent. Thank you."

Dave looked at Elizabeth who rolled her eyes. *That's a surprise. Not bad for an opening statement. There may be more to Buttress than we think.*

"Would councilors come forward and enter evidence they wish to stipulate?"

I entered into evidence FEMA's National Incident Management System, Rocky Butte County Emergency Plans,

County policies, the coroner's and Sheriff Departments' official Incident reports, and a report written by Dr. Montgomery. I discussed each exhibit.

I entered a document of my plan to have Steve give a demonstration.

Dean Buttress objected.

The Judge said, "I will study the plan and rule on the demonstration when it comes up in the trial."

Dean Buttress offered no evidence to be stipulated.

At four-thirty, the court adjourned.

On the way home, Elizabeth observed, "Judge Cartwright helps us generate a lot of billable hours in a single court day. I'm tired."

At the old Williams place, we gave our car to Cody, who wore slacks, tie, and blue dress shirt, matching mine.

I can't get over how much he looks like me.

We joined Buster in his pickup. Elizabeth whispered, "I'm now really in the big-time."

Inside the lodge, Raven, who had been talking to Candice, enthusiastically greeted me. Peter Gallagher had also flown in.

Over wine and cheese served by Sofia, I related the day's trial proceedings.

After a supper with lots of good conversation, Elizabeth, Candice, Peter, and I moved to the study to go over testimony.

Elizabeth produced her laptop and opened the reporter's dispatch to Danae reporting on the trial. She read for a while. "Boss, here is what she said about you:

It took me a long time during jury selection to figure out that Mr. Willard was not a local country lawyer. He did a good act of 'I was raised in a small town like this and am a country boy at heart . . . and we need to use our horse sense in trying this case.'

However, when he questioned witnesses, I could see the razor-sharp mind of a lawyer from a long letterhead law firm coming through . . . ."

16

THE SECOND DAY

At eight-thirty, The Bailiff ushered the jury into their seats. He disappeared through a door behind the judge's bench and returned. "All rise. Department Three of the Superior Court of Rocky Butte is now in session. Judge Jeremiah Cartwright presiding."

The judge entered.

"Be seated. Good morning, ladies and gentlemen. Continuing the case of Edward and Ann Sodastrom versus The County of Rocky Butte and Sheriff Alfred Bogend. Plaintiff call your first witness."

"I call Ed Sodastrom."

He raised himself from behind our table and shuffled to the witness box in his dark suit and black tie. His white shirt was two sizes too large in the neck. He looked tragic as the Bailiff swore him in.

I stood at the table. "Ed, would you tell the court about April 2, the night Lucy died. 'We were on our way home from visiting friends and stopped to have dinner at the Rawhide Cafe. A light snow fell. While Ann and I were finishing dinner, Lucy asked if she could make a snowman behind the cafe. We told Lucy to stay close and not go near the creek. We finished dinner, and I left the table to get Lucy."

I turned toward the Jury. "How long was it after Lucy left the table?"

"Five, maybe ten minutes."

"Ed, please continue."

"She wasn't in back the cafe. I found her half-finished snowman and tracks in the snow. It looked like she may have been chasing a rabbit because her tracks zig-zagged across the bridge. They disappeared in the falling snow. I searched and called. I told Ann to call 911.

"Sheriff Bogend and his deputy arrived at about a quarter after six. After a brief look-around, he called the county for assistance in a full-scale search. He put us in a booth in the cafe while they warmed up the filling station office next door. By seven, search teams, paramedics, and communications equipment arrived. They moved us to the filling station office where we could be alone."

"Could you tell what was going on from the office?"

"Yes, it had windows in front so we could view what was going on in the parking lot. A window on the side faced the entrance and inside of the Rawhide. The door in the back had a window that looked out toward the creek."

"What happened next?"

"About seven o'clock a man with a bloodhound on a leash knocked. He asked whether we had any clothing of Lucy's. I gave him her extra sweater, and he let the dog sniff. The dog searched around in front of the cafe for a short time, and they ran around back. I stood by the window in the back door and saw the man and his dog headed down Bear Creek Trail on the other side of the creek. Sheriff Bogend came out of the cafe and shouted at the man. After some discussion with the Sheriff, the man and his dog returned to the parking lot.

"Around eight thirty, Steve Manteo arrived on the scene."

"Mr. Sodastrom how did you know it was Mr. Manteo?"

"We didn't know. He introduced himself to Ann and me at Lucy's funeral."

"What made you notice Mr. Manteo?"

"He was not wearing heavy clothing like everyone else. He talked to the deputy outside the cafe and then marched inside to the Sheriff. We watched him because we thought he might have news. Sheriff Bogend looked angry and had his deputy escort Mr. Manteo back to the parking lot.

"Mr. Manteo talked to men of the County Search and Rescue team who showed him the photo of Lucy. Mr. Manteo walked to his car and sat for a minute. He got out of the car and ran back to the deputy who was standing outside the cafe door. They spoke for a few seconds and then Mr. Manteo pushed the Deputy out of the way and rushed to the map on the wall. He marked something on the map as the Sheriff shouted at him. A deputy took Mr. Manteo by the arm and led him out of the cafe."

"What happened next?"

"Mr. Manteo talked to and argued with several of the men in orange vests. He passed behind the cafe and over to the foot bridge where he talked to Deputies. He came back in a few minutes walking bent over with his arms crossed on his chest. Mr. Manteo had sat in his car for a few minutes and drove away."

Ed crossed his arms over his chest as if trying to hold himself together. "At eight o'clock, a Deputy drove us home because we were cold. Ann was collapsing.

"After two a.m. a deputy came to our house and told us they found Lucy and that she had passed away."

Both Ed and Ann Sodastrom, along with several members of the jury, were weeping, The judge called a ten-minute recess.

After the recess, Mr. Buttress cross-examined Ed. "Were you acting as responsible parents when you let your daughter leave the restaurant to play unattended in a snowstorm?"

"Yes, she was only going to be twenty feet away. It wasn't what I'd call a snowstorm. Only a quarter inch of snow had fallen. She had often played there. She knew to never go near the creek or across the foot bridge. She always minded."

"How far is the creek and bridge from the restaurant?"

"About a hundred yards, I reckon."

"Mr. Sodastrom, were you having an argument with your daughter at the time that caused her to run away?"

"Absolutely not."

"Then, why did she run away?"

I jumped to my feet. "Objection your Honor. It has not been established that she 'ran away.'"

"Sustained. The jury will disregard the question, and it will be stricken from the record."

Buttress smiled and seemed pleased with himself.

"No further questions your Honor."

Ann Sodastom wept into her handkerchief.

Judge Cartwright adjourned the court for a fifteen-minute recess.

When we reconvened, The judge asked, "Would the plaintiff like to question the witness on redirect?"

"Yes. Mr. Sodastrom is there anything you would like to add?"

"This case is not about money for us. We have all we need. We want to ensure that in the future, all possible resources, including psychics will be used in searching for lost children."

Dean Buttress stood. "I object."

Judge Cartwright interrupted, "Sustained."

"Is there anything else?"

Ed wiped his eyes. "We shouldn't have to be here." He slumped in his chair with his arms hanging at his sides.

After a long pause, I said, "Thank you."

"I call Marylin Askey."

She came forward and was sworn and seated.

She was forty-something and wore a plain brown dress. Her hair was peroxide-blond.

"Ms. Askey, were you at the Rawhide Cafe on the night of April 2 of this year?"

"Yes. I am the waitress there."

"Did you see the Sodastroms and Lucy that night?"

"Yes."

"Did Lucy argue with her parents?"

"No, she was happy. I gave her a cookie before she went outside. She skipped through the parking lot eating her treat."

"Would you describe the area behind the Cafe?"

'There is a ten-space paved parking lot that belongs to the restaurant. Between the lot and the pedestrian bridge over the creek, the field is graded and paved with gravel."

"Why is it paved with gravel?"

"It belongs to the fancy camp down in Sheffield Valley. Visitors to the camp park their cars there and hike to the camp."

"Were there any cars parked behind the cafe on the night of April 2?"

"Only mine by the back door. The camp is only open during the warm months. There were no other cars there when I left to go home."

"What time was that?"

"About nine-thirty. After the Sheriff had taken over the cafe, I stayed to serve cups of coffee. The Sheriff's Department food truck showed up, so I went home."

At the evidence table, I picked up a map.

"Do you recognize this map?"

"Yes, that is the map we keep pinned to the wall. People are always asking us for directions to the camp, so we put it up for everyone to study."

"Do you notice anything different about the map?"

"Yes, someone drew a big 'X' on the Bear Creek Trail."

"Do you know when the 'X' was drawn?"

"Sort of. I showed the map and gave directions to a customer during the dinner rush. Maybe it was five-something. There was no mark then."

"No further questions, your Honor."

"Defense may cross-examine." The Judge looked at Buttress.

Dean Buttress stood up at his table and asked the witness, "How can you be sure there was no mark? Could it be that you didn't notice?"

"The customer was a city feller. He wanted to know about fishing in the summer. I pointed out popular spots along Bear Creek. If there was a mark, I sure enough, would have noticed."

"No further questions."

I called Harold Rodgers. He had a lean, up-straight military bearing and crewcut. He was sworn and took a seat.

"Mr.Rodgers. Please tell the court why you happened to be at the Rawhide Cafe on the night of April 2."

"I belong to a volunteer group called Three Peaks County Sierra Rescue. We are expert mountaineers trained in SNR."

"*SNR*. That would be search and rescue?"

"Yes. We have a telephone tree that monitors police reports and directs members to where they might be needed. I received a call on April 2 and drove down from Forest Glen."

"Where is Forest Glen?"

"It is over the county line on Highway 47 in Three Peaks County."

"Mr. Rodgers, how many search and rescue team efforts have you been on?"

"Dozens, I guess."

"Do you just show up and search on your own?"

"No, part of our training is how to work with local authorities."

"How do you do that?"

"California uses The National Incident Management System."

"What is that?"

"It's a way for different fire departments and law enforcement and civilian organizations such as ours to work together in emergencies. We check in with the Incident Commander and obey his direction."

"Who was the Incident Commander in the search for Lucy on April 2?"

"Sheriff Bogend."

"Did you check in with him?"

"Yes, at around seven o'clock. He said, 'Who called you? What the hell are you doing here from Three Peaks County? We don't need your help.' He told me to wait outside."

"What happened next?"

"Another member of the Three Peaks County Sierra Rescue, Tim Donavan, showed up while I waited in the parking lot. While were killing time, we studied a topo map we had of the area. We had heard they were only searching toward Sheffield Valley, so we volunteered to search down stream on Bear Creek.

"Did you specifically offer to search down stream on Bear Creek to the Incident Commander, Sheriff Bogend?"

"Yes."

"How did he respond?"

"He glared at me and then said, 'I told you to wait outside for assignment.'"

"What did you do?"

"I waited in the parking lot until nine o'clock and went home. I figured he was never going to use us."

"How would you rate the organization of the search. From one (totally disorganized) to ten (well-run)?"

"I'd give it a three."

"Thank you, Mr. Rodgers."

Dean Buttress questioned the witness.

"Mr. Rodgers, is it safe to say you had no official reason to be at the Rawhide Cafe?"

"Yes, But . . . ."

Buttress interrupted. "Were you somebody who just showed up?"

"Yes, But . . . ."

"Thank you, Mr. Rodgers." Buttress looked smug.

❄

"I call James Azavedo."

"Why did you go to the Rawhide Cafe on the night of April 2?"

"I'm a retired Deputy Sheriff of Three Peaks County, now living in Rocky Butte. I heard of the SNR operation on my police scanner and drove out there to volunteer to help. I checked in with the I.C., Incident Commander, Sheriff Bogend, at about six-thirty and showed him my training credentials.".

"What are your credentials?"

"When we go to a national school and get certified in skills such as SNR, you get a card you carry in your wallet to show to an I.C. when you report for duty.

"How did The Sheriff respond?"

He told me to wait in the parking lot for assignment."

"Did you receive an assignment?"

"No, I waited until nine and left."

How many SNR incidents have you participated in during your career?"

"Maybe somewhere around twenty."

"How would you rate the organization of the search. From one (totally disorganized) to ten (well-run)?"

"About five."

"Thank you, Mr. Azavedo."

Dean Buttress questioned the witness.

"Mr. Azavedo did any Rocky Butte official call you to the Rawhide Cafe?"

"No."

"Were you somebody who just showed up?"

"Yes, But . . . ."

"Thank you, Mr. Azavedo." Buttress stood with his head high and shoulders back as though he was proud of himself.

I rose. "I call Tim Holtz."

Tim stood tall and lanky. He looked like he could run after his bloodhound for an hour without stopping.

"Mr. Holtz, why did you go to the Rawhide Cafe on the night of April 2?"

"I heard traffic on my police scanner radio about the search. I fed my dog and got in my truck and drove to the Rawhide. I asked around about the search. Somebody pointed out the missing girl's parents sitting in the office. They gave me a sweater that belonged to the girl, and I let my dog smell it. The dog went crazy and pulled me toward the cafe. I didn't check in with the sheriff because the dog was off on a charge on the girl's trail. We galloped across the bridge and started down the Bear Creek Trail. The Sheriff called me back. He accused me of interfering with police work and said he would arrest me if I continued the search. I stood around in the parking lot until it was apparent that the Sheriff would not call on us, and left for home."

"Do you have credentials as a Bloodhound handler and trainer?"

"Yes, my dog and I are trained and certified by the California Bloodhound Association for tracking. We worked seven years off and on for law enforcement agencies in the Sacramento and the Northern California area. "Were you aware of The National Incident Management System?" "Yes, I am trained in in that and know I must obey the Incident Commander, the Sheriff."

"Did you show the sheriff your credentials?"

"I tried to, but all he did was rant threats at me."

"Thank you."

I turned to Buttress and said, "Your witness."

"Mr. Holtz, did a Butte County official call you to the Rawhide Cafe?"

"No, but . . . ."

Buttress interrupted. "Were you somebody who just showed up?"

"Yes, But . . . ."

"Thank you, Mr. Holtz."

Judge Cartwright declared a thirty-minute recess.

Elizabeth and I adjourned to our conference. room.

She opened the picnic basket that Buster had brought in and got a soft drink and an energy bar. "It is going well. I watched the jury. Ed's testimony had a big impact on them. He created a lot of sympathies."

"I'll put Steve Manteo on next while the testimony concerning the Rawhide is fresh in everybody's mind. He has a good story that will fit in with the other testimony. Right now I need to relax."

The judge reconvened the court at eleven o'clock.

He looked at me. "Call your next witness."

"I call Steve Manteo."

17

STEVE'S TESTIMONY

Steve, wore a dark blue business suit with a gray tie. His walk suggested he was confident but not overbearing.

I stood at my table. "Mr. Manteo, tell the court what you do for a living."

"I am a business consultant working out of my home farther up the hill from the Rawhide. My specialty is forecasting the results of business decisions my clients make. I evaluate people who are potential partners or hires."

"How do you do these 'forecasts and evaluations'?"

"I go into meditation and use my psychic abilities to sense current or future situations. The process is called remote viewing."

Elizabeth was carefully watching the jurors and making notes.

"You used the term 'psychic abilities.' Are you a 'psychic' that works in a storefront with a neon sign that says 'fortunes told' or as an advisor to rich people who want to contact their departed relatives?"

"No, I've never done that. I am not a medium; one who allows other voices to talk through them."

"Were you a 'psychic spy' for the Central Intelligence Agency?"

Buttress jumped to his feet and called "Foundation! No basis for being a 'psychic spy' has been laid."

I turned toward the judge. "Your Honor we will now explain the meaning of being a 'psychic spy.'"

Judge Cartwright frowned. I am going to allow it. Please continue."

"Were you a 'psychic spy' for the Central Intelligence Agency?" "The CIA didn't call us 'psychic spies. That's the name authors and publishers used in books written about us."

"Mr. Manteo, How did you become a 'psychic spy'?"

"While an undergraduate at Stanford, I took a psychic aptitude test in a Psychology course. I scored high and was recruited by the Stanford Research Institute. They assigned me to a training program to learn remote viewing."

"Please explain to the court the nature of remote viewing."

"It is the spy craft used by psychic spies. I trained for over a year before being certified for my accuracy. I learned to go into deep meditation and sense what was going on in other places or times."

"Are there others doing remote viewing?"

"Many of the details of the U.S. program are classified. There were many on both sides of the Cold War involved in remote viewing. The U.S. program became declassified in 1995. Many graduates of the classified program published books and offered training in remote viewing methods. There is now a large number of 'second generation' trained remote viewers. Hundreds and maybe thousands of people now do remote viewing.

"How did you know Lucy's location on the night of April 2?"

"Our training in the Government program included locating people."

"Why would the Government want to locate people?"

"I can only talk in hypothetical terms because of classification. U.S. Naval commanders might like to know whether a Soviet Admiral was at a resort on the Baltic or in the Atlantic Ocean commanding a naval task force. The location of American hostages would be important in planning rescue operations."

"When you talked to Sheriff Bogend on the night of April 2, why should he have believed that you could help locate Lucy?"

"I presented him with my credentials folder."

I picked up a copy of Steve's credentials folder from the evidence table. "Is this a copy of the folder?"

Steve examined the folder and said, "Yes."

"Why did you have it with you in the car?"

"I was driving home from a business meeting with a potential client in Sacramento."

"Describe the contents to the court."

"It contains a picture of The President of the United States congratulating me for a remote viewing accomplishment."

"What accomplishment was that?"

"It's classified. All I can say is that it saved many American lives."

"What else is in the folder?"

"Four letters of commendation from high-level officials in the Pentagon, a newspaper clipping about me helping to find lost hikers in the Mount Shasta area, four letters of gratitude from Police Commissioners for solving missing persons cases, and one clipping about me helping solve a murder case."

I spent ten minutes reviewing the contents of his folder.

"Why aren't there letters from your commercial customers?"

"I have confidentiality agreements with my commercial customers."

"Did Sheriff Bogend have this folder in his hands?"

"Yes, but he only thumbed through it and gave it back without reading a single page."

"Then what happened?"

"He ordered a deputy to escort me from the building. I talked to several of the emergency personnel and pleaded for them to search down Bear Creek. They said they couldn't do that unless ordered by the sheriff. I tried to cross the bridge and find Lucy, but deputies stopped me."

"What did you do then?"

"I was cold, so I sat in my car to get warm. I decided there was nothing I could do and then drove home."

"How did you feel about not being able to help Lucy?"

"I went into a state of despair."

The Sodastroms and two members of the jury snuffled into tissues.

Steve sat in the witness box looking distraught.

"No further questions your Honor."

"Would the defense like to examine the witness?"

"Yes, your Honor."

Buttress walked back and forth behind his table with a measured gait like a cat stalking prey.

"Mr. Manteo, had you ever met Sheriff Bogend before the night of April 2?"

"No."

"Then, would you say you were a complete stranger to him?"

"Yes."

"Were you aware of the National Incident Management System adopted by the County and the means of coordinating efforts of civilian organizations and county law enforcement offices?"

"No."

"Have you been trained in the organization and command structure for a Search and Rescue operation."

"No."

Have you ever been called upon by any Rocky Butte County official to assist in any investigation or search?"

"No."

"On the night of April 2, did any official of Rocky Butte County call on you for assistance?"

"No, but. . . ."

"Were you somebody who just showed up?"

"Yes, but . . . ."

Buttress turned toward the Judge. "No further questions, your Honor."

The judge looked at his watch. "Mr. Wellard, redirect?"

I stood. "Yes, your Honor."

"Mr. Manteo, was it your intent in talking to the Sheriff to become a member of a search party?"

"No. All I wanted to do was tell the Sheriff where to find Lucy. I wasn't trained, dressed or equipped to join a search party. Plenty of qualified people stood in the parking lot."

Buttress jumped up. "Objection! Conclusion! Mr. Manteo did not know the qualifications of people standing around."

"Sustained. The jury will disregard the last sentence of Mr. Manteo's testimony."

I looked back at Steve. "You testified you weren't trained, dressed or equipped to join a search party Why did you attempt to cross the bridge and go down the Bear Creek Trail to search for Lucy?"

"I wasn't going to search. I knew exactly where Lucy was, only about a mile away and I would have run most of the way. I was willing to risk getting cold to save her."

"You weren't allowed to cross the bridge by deputies?"

"That is correct."

"Why did you expect the Sheriff to take you, a stranger, seriously when you offered to help?"

"My credentials folder, in his hand at the time, had a picture of The President of the United Stated congratulating me on a Psychic Spy achievement."

"No further questions at this time, your Honor. I reserve the right to recall this witness."

The Judge looked at Buttress. "No, your Honor."

Buttress is doing the right thing. Cross-examining Steve could have backfired on the defense case in many ways

"Call your next witness."

18

MORE TESTIMONY

"I call Deputy Dave Chalmers." As he was being sworn, I noticed he stood as rigid as soldier at attention.

"Deputy Chalmers, were you an official member of the search and rescue team at the Rawhide Cafe on April 2?"

"Yes. I reported from the county's Pine Mountain Sheriff's Station."

"Were you the Search and Rescue Team member who found Lucy?"

"Yes, Along with my partner, Ben Higgins."

"Deputy Chalmers, why was it you and your partner searched downstream on Bear Creek?"

He looked afraid and glanced at the sheriff. "At one-thirty in the morning, the search was about to be called off. I said to Ben, 'I'm freezing. Let's hike down Bear Creek to warm up. I heard a rumor someone saw her there.' My partner said we shouldn't do that without the sheriff's direction. I told him we weren't disobeying the sheriff; we were warming up and staying in shape. We found the girl in a log cabin and called for paramedics on the radio. Regrettably, it was too late."

I picked up the map from the evidence table. "Are you familiar with this map?"

"Yes, that is the map from the wall in the Rawhide Cafe."

"How do you know it's the same map?"'

"It has an 'X' marked at the place we found the missing girl. After Ben and I had got back from down the creek, we filled out reports. I looked at the map to check something, and I noticed the 'X' at the place we found the missing girl. I figured the paramedic with us made the mark."

"Are you positive it's marked at the place you found the missing girl?"

"Yes, a hundred yards up Bear Creek from that old logging railroad trestle."

"Thank you, Deputy Chalmers."

Judge Cartwright's booming voice broke the mood. "The court is adjourned forty-five minutes for lunch."

Elizabeth and I adjourned to our conference room to eat our bag lunches. Elizabeth looked at her sack and took out her sandwich. "Trials in Rocky Butte: the big time. Where is Steve?"

"He and Georgia are having a picnic in the park and going to run an errand. He said he needed space."

"Only a couple more days." I opened my sack.

Elizabeth ate. "Boss, before we came up here, I thought of you as an egghead patent attorney. You're a great personal injury lawyer."

"Thanks. As a bonus, I get my very own stalker. Did you notice the guy with the crewcut gray hair and the gold-rimmed glasses? He's my nemesis."

"Yes, I saw him. I thought he was weird. Not a Rocky Butte local. He had a terrible vibration. He made faces in response to what people said like an undisciplined third-grader. Is that why Buster sat right behind him?"

"Yes, and the other western attired guy sitting two seats away is one of Buster's guys. I'm not worried."

"Boss, what is up for the afternoon?"

"Candice and Peter will say their theory thing. I will finish the day off with the sheriff. We'll let the jury go home with his testimony fresh in mind."

The jury filed back in. The Judge boomed, "Mr. Wellard. Call your next witness."

"I call Dr. Candice Montgomery." Candice walked forward in a long black dress. Her wide, brown eyes sparkled.

"Dr. Montgomery, please tell the court your current employment."

"I'm an Assistant Professor of Mathematics at San Marino State College."

(I spent forty-five minutes reviewing her education and accomplishments to qualify her as an expert witness.)

I walked to the evidence table and picked up a hundred page report. "Dr. Montgomery, you mentioned you have ten years experience in theoretical work in eight-dimensional space. Did you author this report, A Theoretical Explanation of Eight-Dimensional Remote Viewing?"

"Yes."

"Please read the summary from the first page."

"Remote viewers gain information over great distances. This report presents a theory of how this works. The information is limited to low-bandwidth simple descriptions of basic human sensations (e.g., cold, noisy), basic emotional states (e.g., grief, anger, fear), locations (e.g., where a person is), or picture elements (e.g., something big, curves, lines)."

I scratched my head to look confused. "What education level is required to read and understand this report?"

"At least a bachelor's degree in mathematics or physics."

"Should we expect the jury to read and understand the report?"

"No, all they need to know there is a valid scientific explanation of why and how remote viewing works."

"Dr. Montgomery, if a person only wanted to understand a little about remote viewing, what should they read?"

Her eyed opened wider with clear excitement. "Oh, that's simple. If you want to learn more, I wrote an easy-to-understand book with figures."

I went to the evidence table. "Is this the book, *A Friendly Guide to Remote Viewing*?"

"Yes, anyone can read it if they want to understand the basics of the theory."

"Please give us a simplified explanation."

She paused and thought. "Einstein and other famous physicists said 'time is an illusion.' We all are mental space-time travelers. If ask you what you had for breakfast yesterday, you can mentally travel back in time and space and perceive what you had for breakfast. If you had practiced time-traveling, you would sense everything you perceived at breakfast: the smell and taste of coffee, the texture, and crunch of your cereal, how noisy it was, who was there; the whole sensory package.

"You might say this is memory stored in your brain. But, if you added up the number of bits of data you can recall from your lifetime, the amount is huge. Neuroscientists cannot explain where or how all of that information is stored.

In my theory, you don't get the memory from some place stored in your brain. You mentally space-time travel through eight-dimensions and observe the actual event.

With training, you can travel to the future. However, your perceptions are like those you might get looking and listening at a keyhole of a darkened room. With time, you could figure out what was going on in the room.

For locating people, you need a photograph or memory of a person. "Your mind can tune into that person and sense where they are.

"I am not saying that every 'psychic phenomena' works this way. This pertains to remote viewing.

"A neuroscientists might say this is a crazy idea. But, they don't have a better explanation."

204

I glanced at the jury. Several members looked confused.

I stood with my palms turned up. "How much of this does the jury need to understand?"

"Only that it is based on years of research published in scientific peer-reviewed journals."

The jurors looked relived.

Buttress declined to cross-examine.

The Judge declared a fifteen-minute recess.

※

After the recess, I said, "I call Dr. Peter Gallagher."

After he was sworn and seated, I asked, "What is your current professional title?"

"I am a Professor Emeritus in the U.C.L.A. Department of Mathematics."

I spent fifteen minutes questioning Peter's academic credentials.

"Dr. Gallagher, are you familiar with this report, *A Theoretical Explanation of Eight-Dimensional Remote Viewing?*"

"Yes, I have studied it in depth. I find no fault with the report.

"Did anyone else study the report?"

"Yes, two other Professors in the Math Department, a Professor in the Physics Department, and graduate student interested in the subject."

I picked up a document from the evidence table.

"Is this their report?"

"Yes,"

"Please read the title of the document."

"*An Evaluation of A Theoretical Explanation of Eight-Dimensional Remote Viewing* by Candice Montgomery Ph.D."

"Are the authors' names on the cover?"

"Yes."

He read the names and their positions on the faculty of UCLA.

"Please read the first paragraph of that report?"

He read a wordy introduction stating that Candice's report was technically sound.

"In your professional opinion, is Dr. Montgomery's report a technically correct explanation of how remote viewing works?"

"Yes."

"Thank you, Dr. Gallagher."

Buttress declined cross-examination.

19

THE SHERIFF'S TURN

"I call Sheriff Alfred Bogend." The Sheriff walked forward in with an obese person's waddle and his arms barely moving. He bulged in his starched khaki sheriff uniform. He looked defiant as he held his chest out and held his chin up.

I questioned the Sheriff for fifteen minutes regarding his training and experience.

He's slow-witted. I'll annoy him by firing questions at him before he has time to think.

"Were you dispatched to search for Lucy Sodastrom on the night of April 2?"

"Yes, the county 911 dispatcher sent me to the Rawhide Cafe at seventeen-fifty-three . . ."

I interrupted, "That is five-fifty-three p.m.?"

He thought for a while. Yes."

"Where were you when you got the call from the dispatcher?"

"In Bob's Cafe in Rocky Butte having dinner."

"What time did you get to the Rawhide Cafe?"

"My deputy and I got there at six-sixteen p.m."

"How long does it take to drive from Bob's Cafe to the Rawhide?"

"About twelve minutes." The sheriff looked annoyed.

"So you left Bob's Cafe four or five minutes after you received the dispatch call."

The sheriff spoke through clenched teeth. "Yes."

"Did you finish your dinner before you left?"

"Yes. We figured it to be a long night. This was the third time we had searched for this girl."

"Please explain 'the third time'."

"We had search parties called out to find her two times last summer when she disappeared into the forest."

"Why was that important on the night of April 3?"

"Her parents should have kept better track of her."

I looked at the jury.

"This copy of your dinner receipt shows you had pie for desert. Is that correct?"

"Yes."

"Did you order the pie after you received the dispatch call?"

"I don't remember."

"Do you think your deputy will remember?"

The sheriff's shirt is getting wet under the armpits.

"All right, I ordered after the call. But, I ate it fast."

"Would you call a child lost in the snow, in weather below freezing an emergency, even though she had been missing before?"

"Yes."

"Did you order pie anyway?"

"Yes."

I can't believe Buttress didn't prepare this guy to testify better.

"What was the weather at the Rawhide Cafe when you got there?"

"A light snow was falling. It was less than an inch deep. The temperature was twenty-three degrees."

"Who did you first meet there?"

"Ann Sodastrom. She told me that her daughter Lucy had gone behind the Cafe to play in the snow and was missing again. She said Mr. Sodastrom was across the foot bridge over Bear Creek hunting for their daughter."

"What did you do then?"

"My deputy and I crossed the foot bridge and found Mr. Sodastrom on the trail to Sheffield Valley calling for his daughter. He said he followed his daughter' tracks in the snow across the bridge but lost the trail."

"What did you do then?"

"I left my Deputy to continue searching while I returned to our patrol car and called the dispatcher and explained the need for a full-scale search. I told her to mobilize the search and rescue team."

"What time was that?"

The Sheriff took a notebook from his pocket and read his notes. "Six-thirty-one."

"That was fifteen minutes after you arrived. What were you doing for fifteen minutes while the child was lost in the freezing cold?"

The sheriff glared at me as he spoke. "I had to walk back to the patrol car and study a map and assess the situation."

"Were you carrying a hand-held radio with you when you met Mr. Sodastrom ?"

"Yes."

"When you first talked to Mr. Sodastrom wasn't it apparent that his daughter was missing?"

"Yes, she was missing again."

"Did you discuss, in your words, 'missing again' with Mr. Sodastrom?"

"Yes, I pointed out to him this was the third time we had searched for this girl."

"Couldn't you call the dispatcher on your hand-held radio?"

"Yes, but I needed to study a map to make a plan for a search."

"Why did you need a plan before you talked to the dispatcher?"

"It was Sunday night. I didn't want to call a bunch of people out unnecessarily."

I paused to make sure the jury got that.

"Would you need to pay them overtime if they are not on duty and you call them out on a Sunday?"

Good. He is looking flustered.

"Yes, also, they have families."

"So, you didn't want to pay overtime or inconvenience personnel by calling them to duty."

"That's not right . . . ."

I interrupted. "Is this your incident report signed by you?" I handed him a copy from the evidence table. "It says you were the Incident Commander. Is that correct?"

"Yes, I was the I.C."

"Does that mean you were in charge and solely responsible for directing the search according to the County adopted National Incident Management System?"

The Sheriff's nostrils flared.

"Yes."

"Do you have training credentials for operating as an I.C.?"

"Yes, I attended a week-long training program in Quantico, Virginia. A card in my wallet says so."

"As I.C., did you direct where the search teams went?"

"Yes."

"Was it your decision to only search the trail to Sheffield Valley?"

"Yes."

"Why did you make that decision?"

"There was a radio report from a search team they had found tracks."

"Did you personally hear the report?"

"No, one of my deputies heard it and informed me."

"After you received the report did you talk to the person who saw the tracks?"

"No."

"Was there a reason you didn't talk to him to verify what he saw?"

The Sheriff scowled. "Yes, I didn't know who radioed the report." His face reddened.

I'm making progress here.

"Did you decide to search only the trail to Sheffield Valley solely on the basis of that second-hand report from an unknown person?"

"Yes, I didn't have unlimited personnel to search everywhere."

"Were there two volunteers from the Three Peaks County Sierra Rescue in the parking lot who volunteered to search the Bear Creek Trail?"

"Yes."

"Why didn't you use them? "

He glared at me. "I worked with some of those people from Three Peaks County before. They think they know everything and are hard to manage."

"Did James Azevedo, a retired Deputy Sheriff also volunteer to help?"

212

"Yes."

"Why didn't you use him?"

"He is another one from Three Peaks County."

"In your words, 'he was from three Peaks County would have thought he knew everything and been hard to manage?'"

The Sheriff paused. "Yes."

What a bozo!

"Did Mr. Holtz and his bloodhound come to the Rawhide during the time you were searching?"

The Sheriff squinted at his notes. "Yes, at seven-fourteen."

"Where did you first see him?"

"I looked out the cafe window and saw him and the dog running downstream on Bear Creek Trail. I ran out of the cafe and shouted for him to stop doing an unauthorized search and report to me."

"What did he say when you talked to him?"

The Sheriff raised his chin in a defiant gesture. "He said he didn't check in because the dog was hot on the trail of the missing girl."

"Why didn't you let Mr. Holtz continue the search?"

"I had summoned a Bloodhound tracker in Pine Mountain. The county has a contract with him."

"Did he arrive and join the search?"

"By the time he arrived, the snow was deep, and the dog couldn't pick up the track."

"Why didn't you use Mr. Holtz and his dog before the snow got deeper?"

"He wasn't a county contractor."

"Why is that a problem?"

"I'd have had to fill out a lot of damn paperwork to justify the expenditure. We already had a tracker under contract."

"Would that be inconvenient?"

"You're damn right. You've no idea how much paperwork has to be filled out after an incident such as this."

"Did Mr. Steve Manteo show up and tell you where the missing girl could be found?"

"Yes, but I didn't know him from Adam. He claimed a magical power to predict where she was?"

"Did he specifically say he had a magical power?"

"I don't remember. There was a lot going on."

"Did he present you with any credentials?"

"No."

"What did he suggest to you?"

"He said I should send deputies on a wild goose chase down the Bear Creek Trail to a place he marked on a map."

I picked up the map from the evidence table. "Is this the map?"

"Yes."

"Where did he mark it?"

"This 'X' here, on the Bear Creek Trail."

"Was that where the missing girl was eventually found?"

"Yes." He loosened his collar and rolled his head.

"You stated that two volunteers from the Three Peaks County Sierra Rescue volunteered to search down the Bear Creek Trail. Is that correct?"

"Yes, but . . . .'

"You stated that you called Mr, Holtz and his Bloodhound back from searching down Bear Creek. Is that correct?"

The Sheriff spread his arms and grasped the edge of the witness box.

"I just told you. He wasn't county contractor . . . ."

"Please answer the question."

"Yes. Damn it."

"Did you testified that you wanted to avoid budgetary and administrative paperwork resulting from utilizing these men?"

The Sheriff turned red, and he lunged up and slapped his hip where his pistol holster would have been if he had been wearing his service belt and shouted, "We've good people in my department. Search and rescue is a job for my people on the county payroll."

There was a long, silent pause as the Sheriff looked around the court.

Jury members looked stunned. One cringed.

"No further questions, your Honor."

The judge looked shocked. He glanced at his watch. "It's now four-twenty. We will continue testimony tomorrow at eight-thirty. Court adjourned."

Bang! Went his gavel.

When we in our car Elizabeth scooted to near the door. "Boss you were vicious. You were getting to him. Did you notice the bailiff moved closer to the witness box toward the end of Bogend's testimony? He must have anticipated that Bogend was ready to jump out of the box on you."

If he'd had his pistol belt on. I would have been a dead man."

"Mr. S. applauded when the sheriff jumped at you. Buster had to resist taking him down.

"We should put in for hazardous-dusty pay when we get back to the office."

20

DAY 3 OF THE TRIAL

When I walked into the courtroom on Wednesday, I noticed Mr. S. and his chaperones (Buster and his associate) and the woman from San Jose were in attendance.

Elizabeth said, "Several new reporters, identifiable by their laptop computers, are here today. Also, Buster is wearing his pudgy bullet-proof vest."

I noted that there were more spectators in the courtroom. Many dressed like housewives.

Elizabeth looked puzzled. "The local grapevine must have been listening to my cell phone call when I called our witness."

The Judge reconvened the court.

"I call Jill Franklin."

"Ms. Franklin, what is your current employment.

"I'm the Manager of the Rocky Butte County Emergency Services Department."

"Does the County have a written policy to use all available resources in emergencies such as a search and rescue incident?"

"Yes."

"Does that policy include using civilians, not employed by the County?"

"Yes, it's reasonable and on-policy for Incident Commanders to use civilians in search operations."

Good. She knows how to testify.

"Ms. Franklin, is there any problem with paying search professionals who show up, such as Bloodhound handlers, if they later bill you for professional services?"

"Not if their fees are customary and reasonable. We have to get approval for off-budget expenditures, but we do it routinely."

"Thank you."

I wonder if Dean Buttress drank his breakfast today. I'll go for it.

"Ms. Franklin. I'd like to clarify the concept of acting as a reasonable person during an emergency. I understand your family owns a cattle ranch. Is that true?"

"Yes."

"Suppose Rocky Butte County was in the middle of a drought, and the cattle were dying of thirst."

Why is Buttress not objecting to a hypothetical situation?

"Furthermore, suppose you had a water well drilling rig on your property. Then, a man who claimed he was a water dowser showed up and said he had dowsed your property and that water could be found if you drilled a well at the far end of your corral. Wouldn't a responsible person who might or might not believe in dowsing, drill the well at the end of the corral if it didn't cost too much?"

Amazing, Buttress is letting me get away with this.

She responded, "Yes, I'd be irresponsible if I let our cattle die of thirst because I didn't believe in dowsing."

"The person should act?"

She looked stern. "A reasonable person should take action."

"Thank you. No more questions."

Judge Cartwright adjourned court for a fifteen-minute recess.

We returned to our conference room. Elizabeth shook her head in disbelief as she took a bottled water from our cooler. "I can't understand why Buttress sat there while you drilled hypothetical wells. Amazing!"

"Maybe somebody snuck in and replaced the defense attorney with a mannequin."

Court reconvened. "I call Janice Silver."

She was a thirty-something looking lady, with long straight brunette hair, dressed in a modest sundress.

"Ms. Silver, please explain to the court how you know me."

"My friend, Ann Sodastrom, called me and asked me to organize a child-finding demonstration for the court. My daughter Kerri is, or was, in Lucy's grade, and I am friends with the mothers of the school class."

Dean Buttress jumped to his feet and objected, "One of the main issues in this trial is scientific credibility. A simple demonstration isn't scientific proof of the legitimacy of psychic phenomena."

Buttress is awake now.

Someone in the spectator section said something and applauded.

The Judge banged his gavel and said, "Order! Spectators will refrain from responding, or I will clear the court."

Elizabeth handed me a note. "Mr. S."

I looked at the Judge. "Your Honor, the scientific credibility of 'psychic phenomena,' in general, isn't an issue in this trial. The issue is limited to Mr. Manteo's ability. This demonstration works toward that end."

"Overruled. I'll allow it. I'd like to see this myself. Please continue Ms. Silver."

I looked at the geologist in the jury He was nodding his head in agreement.

"I'm the president of the PTA, and Ann thinks I'm a good organizer. She gave me your phone number and asked for me to call you in Los Angeles. During that call, you asked for me to get three other parents of children in Lucy's class to take part in the child-locating demonstration. All they had to do was hide with their daughters in separate locations somewhere in town. As instructed, I sent you an email when I had arranged for three girls."

"Did you name the girls or the parents in that email?"

"No."

"Have I or any other person, other than the parents taking part in this demonstration, contacted or talked to you about this demonstration since my first call?"

"The phone call to L.A. is my only contact with you before now. The other attorney, that woman over there, Elizabeth McKenzie, met with me and gave me written instructions."

I went to the evidence table and picked up a document and gave it to Ms. Silver.

"This is Exhibit P-1. Are these the instructions you received from Elizabeth McKenzie?"

She put on her glasses and examined the document.

"Yes. I initialed them at the bottom of the page."

"Please read it aloud to the court?"

She read: "Please contact three other parents of children in Lucy's class willing to be part of a one-hour demonstration. Only you and those other parents are to know of the plans. They should give you a copy of their children's classroom portrait, taken last spring when they had 'picture day' at the school. During the Sodastrom versus County of Rocky Butte trial, you will call each of the other three parents and ask them to wait at their homes for a Deputy Sheriff to come to their house and then go somewhere of the parent's choosing in Rocky Butte. Each location should have strong visual clues you'd recognize if given a photo of that place.

The deputies will to serve as witnesses to verify the demonstration is not rigged. They will give the parents temporary, disposable, "burner" cell phones. Parents are not to carry other cell phones or electronic devices. You are not to inform the deputies of your selected location until you get there. The parent and child should stay at that location for one hour, or until they receive a call, They and their daughters may engage in any activity to entertain themselves while they are waiting for the call."

Ms. Silver put down the instructions, removed her glasses, and sat upright, Did anyone else give you instructions?"

"No."

"Has anybody told you where the three girls are hiding?"

"No."

"I got three pictures from the evidence table, Here are Exhibits P-14, P-15, and P-16." Are these photographs of the three children who are taking part in this demonstration?"

"Yes."

"Please examine them. Are there any markings that might be a clue to the location of the child?"

She looked at them, turning them over and looking at both front and back. "None."

"Please write the name of the child on the back of each picture."

She wrote on the back of each picture.

I turned back to her. "Do you know Mr. Steve Manteo?"

"No, I've never met or had any contact with him."

"Thank you for your help in setting up this demonstration."

"No more questions, Your Honor.

"Mr. Buttress, your witness." The judge looked at his watch.

Buttress stood for a few seconds. "No questions your Honor."

The judge turned to Ms. Silver, "You're excused."

"I call Steve Manteo."

He wore a gray business suit and blue tie. He smiled and looked at the jury.

I handed the three pictures to Steve. "Here are three photos of classmates of Lucy's marked as Exhibits P-14, P-15., and P-16. Their names are on the back. Are you acquainted with any of these children or any families with the same surname?"

I looked at the juror, Ms. Winters. She was sitting upright on the edge of her seat looking interested.

Steve examined the photos. "No. I haven't had contact with any of them."

I gave him a map marked Exhibit P-17 of Rocky Butte and the surrounding area. "These children are somewhere in the vicinity of Rocky Butte. Will you please mark on the map where you perceive the three children to be and describe what each of the children is doing?"

This is this could make or break this case. Will he get them right?

Steve took the first photo in both hands, studied it, and then closed his eyes. The courtroom was silent. The tension built. Steve opened his eyes and turned the picture over, read the name, marked an 'X' on the map, closed his eyes. "Kerri Legar is in a building. She's near a high arched window.and feeling unhappy. I can perceive that she's on the second story, looking out of the window at something moving by."

Good work Steve. One down.

He took the next picture, read the name, closed his eyes for a while, marked the map, closed his eyes again. "Annie Archer is outdoors playing. She's happy, having fun. She's going back and forth . . . on a swing. She's at the school, at the edge of town, on the playground." Steve marked another 'X' on the map.

Hooray! Two down.

The audience murmured, Mr. S. groaned, and Judge Cartwright picked up his gavel.

Steve took the third picture.

The audience grew quiet.

He looked at the third picture, closed his eyes. "Janet Nestle, is here," as he marked another 'X' on the map and then again closed his eyes. In a minute, he added, "Janet is enjoying something cold to eat. She isn't inside but under a blue roof or arbor. There is a blue structure nearby. There are objects . . . cars are going by. She's at the Tasty Freeze on the edge of town."

The courtroom was silent. The jurors were staring at Steve. Four had their mouths open.

I had arranged for the court clerk to have a speakerphone on her desk. She had the numbers of the three disposable phones.

I said, please call any of the three phone numbers. She dialed the first. The jury, heard a male voice answer. "Hello, Richard Lugar here."

"Mr. Legar, this is David Willard calling from the courthouse. Where are you? Is Karri with you?"

"I'm in the library on the second floor. Kari is looking out the window. She is bored and driving me nuts. Can we go home now?" Richard Legar sounded stressed.

"In a minute. Do you or Kari have cell phones or any other electronic devices such as iPhones or tablets with you?"

"No, I was told to leave all electronic devices at home."

"What device are you talking on now?"

"The disposable phone that Deputy Salto lent me."

"One more question: What shape is the window?"

"It's a floor-to-ceiling window with an arch-shaped top."

"Thank you. Your service to the court is appreciated. Please give the cell phone to the deputy.

"Deputy Melanie Soto here, sir."

I asked, "Deputy, are you, Kari and Mr. Legar on the second floor of the library by a high-arched window?"

"Yes, Sir."

"Is the phone you are talking on the one given to you by Elizabeth McKenzie?

"Yes, she gave it to me at the sheriff's annex."

"Have you seen anything during your participation in this demonstration that has made suspicious that an attempt was being made to fool or trick you?"

"No, I didn't know what this was about until you called.

"Please note the time and bring the cell phone to the courtroom and wait to be called to testify."

"Yes, sir."

"Thank you."

I asked the clerk to call the second phone number.

Joyce Archer answered, and reported that her daughter, Amie, was at the school, playing on the swings.

She was with Deputy Sam Frances. I asked him the same questions I had asked Deputy Salto and got the same answers. I instructed him to note the time and bring the cell phone to the courtroom.

The clerk called the third number. Dorothy Nestle stated that she and her daughter, Janet, were at the Tasty Freeze on the edge of town. She was with Deputy Richard Williams who verified their location, replied to the questions I had asked Deputy Salto, and agreed to come to the courtroom.

Good. My pulse is dropping, and my adrenaline is fading.

I entered into evidence the map Steve had marked and then showed it to the jury. "You can see that Mr. Manteo drew three 'X's on the map; one at the library, one at the school playground and one at the Tasty Freeze. Note that he wrote the first name of the child at each location."

"Your Honor, I request recess of ten minutes to allow the deputies to come to court."

"Granted!"

Elizabeth turned. "Mr. S. was making a lot of faces during Steve's testimony. Buster was ready to pounce if needed.

Court reconvened.

Elizabeth handed me a note that read, "Call Deputy Melanie Salto first. She looks eager to testify."

I call Deputy Melanie Salto.

"Deputy Salto, Did you met with my assistant Elizabeth Mc Kenzie at the sheriff's annex this morning?".

"Yes."

"Did she give you a disposable cell phone in the manufacturer's sealed plastic packaging?"

"Yes."

Did you observe her unwrap the phone and go through the setup procedure?"

"Yes."

"Did the phone have GPS or any other location determining capability?"

"No."

"How do you know it didn't?"

She sat up straight in her chair and said with some apparent pride, "At the law enforcement academy I attended, we learned that disposable phones like this one are used by criminals such as drug dealers to avoid being located."

"What instructions did Ms. McKenzie give to you?"

"She gave me a residential address to go to. I was to leave my radio and cell phone and any other electronic devices at the sheriff's annex, drive my personal auto to the residence, and introduce myself. A person at that address would have further instructions."

"What happened then?"

"When I got to the address, Richard Legar met me and asked me to accompany him on a short trip. As requested, I gave him the disposable cell phone."

"What happened then?"

"He drove his daughter Kari and me to the Library. We went to a reading area on the second floor. Kari looked at books but then got bored and said she wanted to go home."

"Did you communicate your location to anyone before Mr. Legar received his phone call from the court?"

"No."

"When did Mr. Legar receive a call?"

She looked at her watch. "Twenty-three minutes ago."

"Do you verify Mr. Legar's statement you were at the library on the phone?"

Dean Buttress jumped up. "Your Honor, objection, hearsay."

"Sustained."

Someone in the spectator section said something and applauded.

The Judge banged his gavel and said, "Order! Spectators will refrain from commenting, or I will clear the court."

Elizabeth scrawled Mr. S. on her notepad and showed it to me.

"Deputy, did you observe Mr. Legar in the second-floor reading room of the library talking on the cell phone you provided twenty-three minutes ago?"

"Yes."

"Did you talk to me on that same phone after Mr. Legar spoke."

"Yes."

"Do you have the phone you used.

"Yes."

"I enter this disposable phone into evidence."

I got the map Steve had marked.

"This is Exhibit P-15, a map of Rocky Butte and the area. Deputy Salto, would you identify the location of the Library you spoke from on this map?"

She studied the map. "It is right here. Someone has marked an 'X' where the Library is."

"Please place your initials by that 'X.'"

The juror, Mr. Segar was noting his head in agreement.

I looked at Buttress, "Your witness."

He stood and looked at the deputy and looked smug. "How can you be sure this is the same phone and not another one switched when you weren't looking?"

She smiled. "Before I left the annex, I scratched an "S" in the case. I checked before I gave it to Mr. Willard just now. My mark was on the case."

Buttress looked disappointed "No further questions."

I called Deputy Sam Frances and asked him the same questions. He answered were similar to Deputy Salto's and he testified. He observed Annie Archer playing on a swing at the school on the edge of town at the time Ms. Archer received the call. He identified where the school was on the map and that there was an 'X' marked there and Annie's name. She placed her initials next to it.

Buttress declined cross-examination.

"I call Deputy Richard Williams."

I asked him the same script of questions, and he gave the expected answers and testified he saw Janet Nestle eating a tasty freeze cone in the shade at the Tasty Freeze at the time I called.

"What color is the cover of the shade structure?"

"Blue, same as the Tasty Freeze building."

I showed him the map exhibit P-15. He stated that the Tasty Freeze was at the 'X' marked on the map by Janet's name. He placed his initials near the 'X.'

"Your Honor, the Plaintiff rests it's case."

The judge declared a forty-five-minute recess.

As the jurors filed out, All took a look at Steve Manteo who was then sitting in the first row in the spectators' area. Some smiled.

21

THE DEFENSE

After lunch, the defense presented its case. Dean Buttress called his scientific expert witness, an Emeritus Physics Professor, Charles Young. He was a gentle, kind looking man from the Bowdon College of California. He gave the expected testimony that there was no scientifically accepted way for Lucy to communicate her position or feelings to Mr. Manteo over two miles away.

I cross-examined. "What year were you awarded your Ph.D.?"

"1970."

"When did you publish you last scientific paper?"

"About fifteen years ago."

"In lay terms, what area of physics did you specialize in?"

"Materials used in semiconductors: transistors, etc."

"Would you say you have kept up with recent advances in physics?"

"Only on my specialty."

"Would that include information transfer in eight-dimensional space?"

He looked puzzled.

"No. But I am familiar with the principals or fields as described by Maxwell's equations."

"When did Maxwell publish his equations?"

"I don't know."

I walked to the evidence table and picked up a document. "This is Exhibit P-22, a copy of *A Dynamical Theory of the Electromagnetic Field* published in 1865 by James Clerk Maxwell. Is this theory, you are referring to?"

"Yes," He looked embarrassed.

"Is it possible that other theories published in the last 150 years might explain Mr. Manteo's abilities?"

Buttress jumped up. "Objection, Your Honor. The question calls for a conclusion."

"Sustained."

"Your Honor, no further questions."

Why did Buttress put such a poorly prepared witness on the stand?

Dean Buttress called Altos Kozinsky. He described himself as president of the Sacramento chapter of an organization dedicated to exposing frauds in claims of paranormal experience. He cited a study that surveyed police departments of the sixty largest cities in the United States and Canada. The published report claimed only forty percent of them ever used psychics, and none reported having received information of great value.

Buttress got Exhibit D-15 from the evidence table. "Is this the report you are referring to?"

"Yes."

In cross-examination, I asked Mr. Kozinsky what his profession was.

"Real estate broker."

"Did you study science in college?"

"No, I didn't go to college."

"When was the study, exhibit D-15, you described published?"

"I don't know."

He sat up straight like. He was proud to answer.

I got the report from the evidence table. "Is this the report you are referring to?"

"Yes."

"Please read the date shown on the cover."
"1973."

I've got him.

"Have you seen any similar studies done after this one in 1973?"

"No."

"Was it published in a peer-reviewed journal and reviewed by other scientists?"

"Not that I'm aware of."

"Who published the study?"

"Our organization."

I'm home free.

"The organization you described as dedicated to 'exposing frauds in claims of paranormal experience'?"

"Yes."

"Besides being 'dedicated to exposing frauds in claims of paranormal experience' what were the author's academic credentials?"

"He didn't show them."

"Was Mr. Manteo mentioned specifically in the study?"

"Not that I remember."

"Does this study have anything to do with Mr. Manteo?"

"Yes, it shows that all psychics are frauds."

You are a dream witness.

There was a murmur among the spectators. The Judge banged his gavel. "Quiet."

"I recall Professor Charles Young."

Dean Buttress looked as though he wanted to object but couldn't think of why.

I asked Professor Young to listen while the clerk read back the questions and answers of my cross-examination of Altos Kozinsky. "From the testimony you heard, does this study provide scientific proof–according to academic standards–that it was impossible for Mr. Manteo to discern Lucy's location?"

Professor Young looked embarrassed as he answered, "No."

"Thank you."

Dean Buttress rested his case.

Judge Cartwright picked up his gavel. "I'll hear closing arguments tomorrow morning. This court is adjourned."

Bang!

22

TROUBLE

As we descended the courthouse steps, reporters pushed microphones in our faces and shouted questions. We responded, "No comment," and explained that Judge Cartwright had asked us not to comment on the case to the media. Both Elizabeth and I noticed that a TV reporter had Janice Silver on camera in an interview. She looked authoritative as she answered questions.

As we drove back to the ranch, Elizabeth said, "We finally hit the big time. Reporters and TV cameras asking questions. How did you like my 'no comment' speech? I've been rehearsing it."

"Clarence Darrow couldn't have done it better."

We got to the old Williams place, gave Cody the car, and joined Buster in his pickup.

When we arrived, Raven and Sofia were sitting on the porch, sipping wine.

As I got out of the car, Raven, dressed in a white jogging suit, ran over and gave me a welcoming kiss, stepped safely away and executed a series of punches in the air, orchestrated by guttural "Yah, Yahs," and made a head kick in the air. "He-ah!" Sofia was standing nearby, laughing.

"I can tell you ladies didn't spend the day sitting on the porch embroidering doilies."

"Go ahead, big boy, make your move!" snarled Raven.

Buster stepped forward. "I think we should change the topic of conversation."

"All of our witnesses have gone home. Steve went up the hill after his testimony and everyone else left on the afternoon plane. We've got the place to ourselves."

Elizabeth interrupted, "I can use a good kick in the head about now. Do you have any whiskey in the house?"

When we got to the old Williams place Thursday morning, Cody was not there to switch cars with us. There were several other dark-colored vehicles in the driveway near the house.

Buster said, "I'm driving you to court today. Cody is okay. Everything is fine; our worries concerning Mr. S. are gone. I'll brief you later when I know more."

Judge Cartwright called the court to order and asked for my closing argument.

After I had given mine, Dean Buttress gave his. The Judge gave the jury their deliberation instructions.

The jury filed out of the courtroom. The court adjourned at eleven o'clock.

Elizabeth watched the jurors leave and then commented, "We're in good shape. The jurors who looked at Buttress did so in apparent disgust. Several stared pityingly at the Sodastroms. I think they'll elect juror number five as foreperson. He seems a gentle, reasonable man."

We retired to our conference room. I checked my text messages and found one from Zaza. It said, "Highest priority emergency: Call Phil Bracken at once."

I called Phil. "We have a bad situation here. Sam Perris, the Chief Scientist at CharMed, our major client, happened to be in Sacramento yesterday. He said he saw you on the evening news declining to comment on the Rocky Butte case. Then, he saw an interview with a woman who had taken part in some courtroom antic. According to Perris, you put on a rigged demonstration proving that clairvoyance works. Is this true? Perris is threatening to fire us from his case because our firm lacks scientific integrity."

"I had the CIA psychic do a demonstration where he located three children hidden in places outside the courtroom. The demo was not rigged."

Phil replied, "Well, settle the case. I'll take care of Vince Colson. Get it out of the news. We can't afford to lose this client. You realize how important CharMed is to our future."

"It's too late. The case went to the jury this morning. I have no way to find the opposing counsel let alone offer a settlement. The verdict will be back before we could even start negotiations. Too late to trigger a mistrial. The Judge wants this trial over. There is nothing I can do."

Except to hunt for a new job.

Phil still sounded mad when he said, "Well, I'll work on damage control. Goodbye!"

That sounded like a 'goodbye,' don't come home.

"Your face is pale! What was that about?" asked Elizabeth.

When I explained, Elizabeth looked shocked and worried. She peeked contemptuously into her bag lunch. "All this and we also get free sack lunches."

The door opened, and Buster walked in with a picnic hamper.

"No sack lunches today. Since you can't leave with the media out there, Sofia made you something special."

Elizabeth grabbed the hamper and unpacked it with little exclamations of delight.

Buster cheerily announced, "Mr. S. didn't get to come to court today. He's staying with our friends at the FBI. He'll be under their care for a long time."

"Last night Cody was awakened at three o'clock by the infrared perimeter alarm. He checked the surveillance video cameras and saw somebody entering the parking area in front of the house and going over to the Camaro. It was Mr. S., who jimmied the car door open, reached in and popped the hood. Cody woke up Billie, our second man staying at the Williams' house. Our other man, Curt, had been tailing Mr. S. in the woods. They watched as he placed a bomb under the hood and wired it to the starter. Then he taped another device to the bottom of the gas tank. He did a little dance of delight and then went back to the woods.

"Curt was waiting and took him down without a fight. Billie was right there to help. They handcuffed Mr. S. as he screamed and yelled threats. Cody called his FBI contact in Sacramento. A federal marshal came and took Mr. S away. An FBI bomb specialist and an investigative team got to the Williams' place this morning. I joined them there after I dropped you off at the courthouse.

"The FBI disarmed the bombs in the Camero. They took the Camaro away to their evidence lab. Cody left on a fishing vacation. That part of the operation is over, and so is Mr. S.

"Now, let's celebrate the end of Mr. S and the trial." Buster produced four canned martinis and a six-pack of beer from a cooler. "You can have a Beverly Hills attorneys' two-martini lunch."

I may have lost my job. I'm not feeling celebratory.

"Only beer for me, thanks. Martinis are a wonderful idea, but I've email and reading to do."

I'd better start working on my resume.

Elizabeth scooped up the four martini cans into her arms. "I'm through for the day, aren't I, boss?"

I smiled in approval.

Later, the bailiff informed us that the jury was through for the day and that they hadn't reached a verdict. Buster drove us back to the ranch. We drove by the old Williams' place. The Camaro and the other cars were gone. As Elizabeth and I strained our necks to look back, Buster volunteered, "Someone will be up to brief us tomorrow."

When we arrived at the ranch, Raven and Sofia were again sitting on the porch in rocking chairs, wearing prim gingham dresses, apparently knitting. They demurely nodded and said, "Welcome home," without getting up.

"Actors!" spat out Buster as we went in and the screen door slammed behind us. "I'm sorry, Raven may never be the same after Rocky Butte."

I went upstairs and changed into boot-cut Levis and pearl-buttoned Western shirt. When I came down, Raven greeted me with a small curtsy and handed me a tall drink. She said in a southern accent, "A mint julep for you sir, after your hard day's work in the fields." Everyone else was standing, laughing, with juleps in hand.

Elizabeth, looking bleary-eyed, walked in. She opened her laptop and said, "Here's Dave's closing statement as transcribed by the reporter's laptop dictation software. It's part of her report to Danae.

Raven and Sophia started to reach for the laptop.

Elizabeth pulled it back. "I'll save you time and summarize the key points:

"One: The Sheriff ignored the County of Rocky Butte Policy to use all available resources.

"Two: He failed to take action on Steve's telling him where Lucy was, and the corroborating evidence of the Bloodhound following Lucy's track.

"Three: Using psychics is within the standards of conduct of law enforcement agencies.

"Four: A reasonable person would have looked at the credentials of all the volunteers, including Steve's and accepted their offers to help."

Elizabeth paused and looked at Raven who seemed confused.

"It all boils down to the argument that the Sheriff was negligent because was failed to act according to the accepted standards of conduct to do what any reasonable person should do and use his excess personnel to perform an early search down Bear Creek Trail."

Raven looked puzzled. "You mean that was all the trial was about? What about Steve's demonstration and all the science stuff?"

Elizabeth sat down and drooped her shoulders. "All that was to establish Steve's credentials. Also, Colson wanted us to get the science stuff on the record as a precedent that to be used in future trials.

I have a transcript of the defense council's closing argument. It's almost the same as his opening statement.

"I'll pass," said Sofia. Raven nodded in agreement.

The next morning, as I went down for breakfast, Buster asked me to stay at the ranch for a couple of hours. He said someone was coming around ten o'clock to brief me about Mr. S.

Elizabeth volunteered to go to court and be available for jury questions.

I happily agreed to delay going to court and snuck back to bed.

At breakfast, Raven said, "Do you have the letter predicting the outcome of the trial that Steve sent you? You were not going to open it before the trial. Do you want to open it now?"

I thought for a minute. "I don't see why not. Seeing the letter can't change what I did in the trial." I hurried upstairs and retrieved the unopened letter from my bag.

I came back to the table and theatrically paused, opened the letter and held it to my forehead. I started to say, "I predict this letter says . . . ."

Raven laughed, "Open the damn thing!"

I opened it. "I saw a pick."

I handed the letter to Raven.

"What does that mean, 'a pick?'"

"It means Steve foretold us winning the case."

Raven bounced up and down and shouted, "Whoopee!"

When I hadn't joined in, Raven scolded, "After convincing the jury of the validity of Steve's abilities, do I sense disbelief? You hypocrite!"

"Yippee!" I shouted. Raven and I danced around.

"What's going on here?" Sofia demanded as she ran out from the kitchen. "Everything okay? Raven, Is this man bothering you?"

"We won! Dave won the case!"

Sophia looked at her watch. "The court is not even back in session. How do you know the verdict?"

"We were celebrating Steve's Manteo's prediction."

The front door screen banged, and I saw Buster.

"Dave, let's take a ride to the airstrip."

"Okay. Raven, please explain the letter to Sophia."

As we drove to the airstrip, Buster volunteered no information on who the visitor might be.

This is mysterious. I don't need any surprises now.

We heard an airplane in the distance. A black, high-winged, twin turbine jet circled over the strip to check the windsock. It touched down and taxied to us. The company logo painted on the side read *California Energy Transmission*. I was puzzled until Mr. Burton got out. He was wearing a black suit, reflecting aviator sunglasses, and his professional, inscrutable expression. He shook my hand and acknowledged Buster with a nod.

"Mr. Willard, we trust your stay was pleasant and successful, and the arrangements were convenient."

"Yes, Buster made me feel safe and secure."

"Buster has briefed you of Mr. S's. visit the decoy house, his placing of bombs in the car and, his apprehension?"

"Yes, that was good work."

"Mr. S. is being held and will be tried in Federal Court for his activities here and at CrystalSky. He worked alone. You need not worry."

"How do you know he worked alone? Aren't there other members of his organization, Skeptemos, that will want to continue his work of stopping those who would corrupt pure science with metaphysical ideas?"

Burton leaned toward me as if sharing a confidence. "Skeptemos has been on the F.B.I. and Homeland Security's radars for a long time. Their investigators keep tabs on the few members they know might be dangerous. None of them are after you. My contact in the F.B.I. told me in confidence that 'Mr. S.' was their only member with weapons or explosives training."

"With your permission, and the knowledge of Dan, your associate at CrystalSky, we placed your sailplane under surveillance. The video showed Mr. S. entering your sailplane trailer and placing explosive devices in the cockpit. He altered your parachute so that the ripcord wouldn't function."

He put bombs in my sailplane? He was a threat!

"Does the FBI have my sailplane in their big evidence locker with the Camero?"

"No, the FBI evidence team removed the explosives. A FAA aircraft inspector has gone over your airplane to assure its safety and airworthiness. The parachute was examined at the FBI laboratories and then repacked at a certified FAA facility. It's back in your sailplane."

I'm not sure I will be very eager to take off in my sailplane. It is mow a 'flying crime-scene.'

"Your desert home was under surveillance. Neither Mr. S. nor any other person entered your home."

"Is the house bugged now?"

"We removed our surveillance devices. Do you have any other questions?" Burton asked mechanically.

"No," I replied just as mechanically.

"Thank you for your cooperation and indulgence in our assignment." Burton shook my hand, nodded to Buster, and then climbed back into his airplane.

"I'm glad he's on our side," I confided to Buster as it taxied away.

Buster stood as though at attention, like a soldier in a military ceremony, until the jet took off. In the Jeep on the way to the lodge, Buster confided that he had only met Burton in person three times. "Colson is considered an important client of E.B. Services. A lot of deals in the world of venture capital are secretive in nature and the target of international industrial espionage."

"How did I rate Mr. Burton flying up here to check on how well you did your job. Why didn't he use the telephone?"

Buster looked at me while he formed an answer. "A lot of people in the security/bodyguard business come from government covert operations backgrounds. They fear to leave paper or electronic footprints and prefer face-to-face communications. I guess you could call it a spook community cultural convention."

As we drove up to the lodge, Raven and Sofia practiced karate exercises on the lawn.

I said to Buster, "Raven looks like a full–fledged karate expert. How did t she get so good in a few days?"

"Sofia has a black belt. She sometimes teaches at an academy and works with actors preparing for movie roles. She says Raven is a natural. I'd be careful to not get her mad from now on. If you need to argue, do it over the telephone."

"Fair warning. I'll get my briefcase, and we can go into town to wait for the verdict."

"It's okay for you to drive yourself in the SUV. Burton called off the bodyguard detail. I'll go with you. I want to hear the verdict."

At the courthouse, I joined Elizabeth and the Sodastroms in a conference room. Ed Sodastrom asked meekly, "If we win the trial, we'll get money, right?"

"Yes, but the case might get appealed. It will be years before you get a check."

"Well, Ann and I've been talking. We don't need the money. We'd want to create a memorial scholarship fund for the children of Rocky Butte."

"That's a wonderful idea! Our law firm will keep you posted on how the appeals process is going. When we get closer to a final judgment, please contact me. I'll be happy to set up trusts and take care of any agreements that are necessary, pro bono—no charge to you. You and Ann might as well wait at home—we've no idea how long the jury will be out. You're only a few minutes away; we can call you when the jury comes back. Be ready to come on a moment's notice. Elizabeth will call you if the jury doesn't reach a verdict today and goes home for the night."

"Thank you," said Ann. "Ed and I need rest." They left, not walking as bent over or looking so forlorn as they did at the start of the trial.

They are beginning to heal. I've changed during this trial. This trial has been more than just a logic game and billable hours. I am making a difference with my lawyering. I usually represent corporate clients that I don't care about. If I win or lose a case, it only results is a comment in a Board meeting, a footnote in a financial report and a big paycheck for me.

I watched the Sodastroms leave.

I helped them gain closure. From now on. The Sheriff's Department will do Search and Rescue operations differently.

That's good.

There is now a legal precedent that many county counsels will notice. Vince Colson has furthered his objective of legitimizing the use of psychics.

I had another important realization.

This experience resolved a major conflict about psychic stuff between Raven and me.

Buster came into the conference room. "Sofia called and asked if the girls can come into town and eat lunch with us."

"That's a great idea. The bailiff is taking the jury to Bob's Cafe so we can't go there. I'm not sure we trust the food at the other restaurant. Then there is the Tasty Freeze."

Buster frowned.

"Tell them to bring a picnic lunch, and we can meet them in Pioneer Park here in Courthouse Square."

"I'll ask Elizabeth to join us. The bailiff showed me a way to go through the new annex and avoid the media."

In the conference room. Buster listened to music, and Elizabeth and I read for a while until my phone rang. I answered and said, "Thank you."

"The jury is going to lunch."

Elizabeth scurried from the room, "I'm going to read the jury. I'll catch up with you at the park."

Buster and I snuck out the back of the annex. In the park, we found Raven and Sofia sitting at a table drinking glasses of wine. They were both again wearing gingham dresses with bows in the back. Plates and a picnic of sandwiches and salads decorated the table.

Sofia must have come to the dude ranch with a whole trunk of costumes from movies.

Buster joked, "You girls will get arrested for drinking in a public park."

They looked at me with puzzled expressions, and I said, "It's okay, I know the Sheriff."

Raven faked a guilty expression, hid her glass under the table. "We don't want to run afoul of the Rocky Butte law."

Sophia put the wine bottle back in the paper sack. "We'll pass it around, taking turns."

Elizabeth arrived. "The jury is in a good mood. Everybody's smiling. They have agreed on something. I sensed they might be debating the penalty now. Boss, can I have a word?" She walked away from the table.

"While I was watching the jurors walk to Bob's Cafe, I saw Mr. Segar, the retired building planner from Three Peaks County look guilty as he removed something from his pocket and threw it in a trash can. When they were gone, I sneaked a peek at what he threw away."

"Elizabeth, I'm not sure I want to hear this for ethical reasons."

"Boss, I understand. I'm under the impression, not borne out by any facts, that he threw away something that looked like a copy of a page from a Three Peaks County Employee Training Manual on employee liability insurance coverage. I only suppose that manual explained that settlement money in a liability case comes from a State Insurance Fund. Money. It's not from the counties' general funds used for paying teachers, keeping the library open, or filling potholes. The jury might be more generous with the award if they knew that."

Elizabeth looked me straight in the eye. "Of course. this is speculation on my part."

"Is the document still in the trash?"

"Yes, as far as I know."

Good! We can only speculate on what Mr. Segar said in the jury room.

It could be grounds for a mistrial if I told the judge. Phil Bracken, and CharMed would like that. But, the Sodastroms would lose out. This is a simple choice

"Elizabeth, since this is only speculation, we should forget what you 'didn't see.'"

Raven handed the wine bottle in the sack to Elizabeth and then stopped and said, "No, we'll risk it and use wine glasses!"

As we were eating, I asked Buster, "What're you going to do next?"

"I've got to get in shape after sitting in a courtroom. We are going up the mountain to camp and hike. Our agent called and said we both have a gig on a movie in the Colorado Mountains for most of September."

My cell phone rang. It was the court clerk saying the jury returned from lunch and was continuing deliberation.

"When will they have a verdict?" Raven asked.

Elizabeth volunteered, "It's Friday afternoon. Two of the jurors play on the Rocky Butte Claim Jumpers' softball team. It has an important league game tomorrow. There'll be a verdict today. They will want to have the deliberation over. "

Raven stood up and brushed crumbs from her gingham dress. "Sofia and I are going to tour the Pioneer Museum and then take in the sights of the town."

Elizabeth, Buster, and I snuck through the annex into the courthouse. In the conference room, Buster sat in one of the antique captain's chairs, rocked back, put in his ear buds, pushed his Stetson over his face and had a nap. Elizabeth and I read. At four o'clock, the clerk called to say the bailiff came out of the jury room to get the formal papers the jury needed to fill out. They will return a verdict soon.

23

THE VERDICT

Elizabeth called the Sodastroms to and asked them to return to court.

Inside the courtroom, tension filled the air. Spectator seats filled. Reporters opened their laptops and talked.

Elizabeth looked around the room. "This must be a big court case for Rocky Butte. Is there time for me to put on my TV interview makeup?"

The Sodastroms joined us in the courtroom, and soon Judge Cartwright appeared and banged his gavel. A hush fell over the court. The jurors filed in. Nobody smiled.

Judge Cartwright asked, "Has the jury elected a foreperson?"

"Yes, sir," Replied juror number five.

"Have you reached a verdict?"

"Yes sir," said the foreman as he handed a piece of paper to the bailiff. The Judge put on his eyeglasses and read the slip of paper. He paused with a look that betrayed disagreement and handed the paper back to the Bailiff.

"Read the verdict," commanded the Judge.

The foreman paused and glanced at the other jurors. They looked timid or embarrassed.

"We find for the Plaintiff."

The jurors broke into smiles.

Noise filled the courtroom.

Judge Cartwright banged his gavel and called, "Order! Order or I will clear this courtroom."

We held our breath.

The jury foreman said in a loud voice, "We award the plaintiff eighteen million dollars."

Chaos erupted in the court. Reporters pushed to leave.

Judge Cartwright stood, banged his gavel and called, "Order! Order!"

The judge thanked the jury. I heard a gasp and turned around in time to see Ed catching Ann.

"I'm okay," she said. "My knees just went weak."

The gavel banged again. "This court is adjourned."

Elizabeth gave me a hug as I stood there stunned. "We did it, boss!"

Ed and Ann Sodastrom cried as they shook our hands. "Thank you! Thank you! The verdict says that pig-headed sheriff was wrong and caused us to lose our Lucy. It also says that nice Mr. Manteo was right in trying to help."

Color had returned to Ed and Ann's faces for the first time since I met them.

I turned to say goodbye to opposing counsel, but he was gone.

I motioned to the Bailiff. "Will you take the Sodastroms out the back entrance to avoid the media and go with them to their car?"

He agreed.

Ann gave Elizabeth and me a tearful hug. "Thank you!" she reiterated as Ed led her off to follow the Bailiff.

Elizabeth and I gathered up our briefcases. Buster led, nudging reporters out of the way as we left the courthouse. On the steps, several reporters and two television crews pushed microphones in front of us. "Mr. Willard! Carol Tipton from NBC. Congratulations! Please comment on the verdict."

"I congratulate the jury for reaching a fair verdict. No amount of money will bring Lucy back, end the Sodastrom's grief, or restore their health.

"This verdict has created a lasting memorial to Lucy: it will put California counties and sheriffs on notice that it is negligent to ignore any reasonable person who claims to have knowledge of where a missing person is, even if they claim to have clairvoyant powers."

Carol was looking around for someone else to interview. "Thank you."

As we continued down the steps, dodging reporters and microphones, Elizabeth quipped, "A press conference after a verdict already. This is more like it.

24

THE CELEBRATION

On the drive back to the ranch I was mentally rehearsing my grand entrance and theatrical announcement. However, when we got back to the lodge, the celebration had already started. Sofia had poured each of us a glass of champagne and greeted us at the door. Raven, dressed in her red gingham dress, ran over and gave me a big kiss and hug. Everyone was jubilant.

"Raven, how did the news of the verdict get here before us?"

"The reporter copied us in the email she sent to Danae announcing the verdict."

After a few congratulatory minutes, Raven and I sat at the table with Sofia who wore her light blue gingham dress. Raven and Sofia were snickering about something, and I sensed it was not the verdict. I noticed that Raven was resting her hand on an ice pack.

Sofia pointed to Raven, "We might have a new client for you: an assault and battery case."

"It was self-defense, perfectly acceptable conduct in the Wild West." Raven looked indignant.

"After Raven and I saw the sights of Rocky Butte we decided we couldn't leave Rocky Butte without a little honky-tonking, so we stopped by the Claim Jumper to have a beer. We were sitting alone at a table, minding our own business, enjoying mugs of Claim Jumper Pale Draft Beer, when Raven excused herself to go to the ladies' room. I heard a commotion and saw a big cowboy sliding down the wall, bent over in pain, holding his bloody nose. I saw Raven disappearing in the hall to the ladies room and watched to make sure she was not followed. I heard a lot of groaning. The cowboy's buddies took the bleeding cowboy away. In a couple of minutes, Raven reappeared walking demurely, as though nothing had happened. The cowboys gave her lots of room to pass."

"He groped me. I hit him reflexively. I didn't even know I did it until I saw his nose and felt my knee in his crotch."

I held my head. "Sofia, you might have created a monster with your karate lessons."

"You should've seen that room full of cowboys. Casting directors couldn't assemble a group as ugly as that. For an instant, I thought the two of us would fight our way out, back-to-back, doing karate kicks. Raven, have you ever thought you might to be a stunt person in the movies?"

"I think I 'd rather deal with Beverly Hills High juniors than make a living doing that."

We laughed and drank more champagne.

Buster's cell phone rang, and he walked outside to take the call. Then he walked down the steps and drove the SUV toward the lake and airstrip.

Steve and Georgia drove up to the lodge and joined the celebration. Steve was beaming. "I knew it would be a win, but not that big. I hope that nobody else will ever have to tell my sad story."

Georgia looked around the room. "Steve said your dark-complexioned lady with black hair is here. I'd like to meet her."

"I'd be delighted to introduce you." I led Georgia over to the table where Raven was sitting. She arose and introduced herself. They seemed to form an instant connection and were soon chatting of metaphysical activities they'd encountered in L.A. I noticed Georgia was giving Raven the stare that meant she was reading her. Suddenly, Georgia broke into a big smile and continued with the conversation.

I turned to Steve. "I was tense during your court demonstration. You acted so calmly. Weren't you nervous performing an on-command demonstration in that environment?"

"I sort of cheated. I meditated the night before and traveled in time to the demonstration. I perceived where each of them would hide and what they would be doing. The only thing I didn't know before the court performance was the names of the children. I rechecked my conclusions during my testimony."

A vehicle made dust coming on the road from the entrance to the ranch. It was a white delivery vehicle. Sofia walked out of the lodge, talked to the driver, and directed him to the kitchen door. She came back in, disappeared into the kitchen, and returned to the living room with a fresh bottle of champagne. "The caterers have arrived."

How could this be?

"From Rocky Butte? That was fast!"

Sofia smiled, "From Sacramento. I placed the order this morning."

"How did you know?" I turned my head in disbelief.

"I called Steve. He said the verdict would come back in the early afternoon. It would be a cause for celebration.

Two minutes later a man and a woman dressed in black uniforms appeared from the kitchen carrying trays of hors d'oeuvres.

Buster drove up in the SUV. Then, to my great surprise, Vince Colson and Danae got out.

I greeted them at the door and received vigorous handshakes and congratulations.

"How were you able to time your arrival to be here at the start of our celebration?"

"Steve had alerted Danae that the trial would be over this afternoon. We timed our flight from a business meeting in LA to Palo Alto so it could divert here when final word came. Our pilots selected a jet they would be comfortable landing on the ranch airstrip.

"We wanted to be here to congratulate you and the whole team. I consider this an enormous win in our crusade to widen the scientific paradigm. My security consultants say we are rid of that Skeptemos guy for good. You know, he put a bomb on one of our airplanes a couple of weeks ago. We have a good surveillance system at our hangar, mostly to know whether somebody places industrial espionage eavesdropping devices on our planes. It works for mad bombers too. Our video surveillance shows it was your guy. That's how we got the FBI involved."

Danae excused herself and went to Georgia and Steve, gave them hugs, and then chatted. I had never seen her enjoying herself before. She was usually all business.

Danae made the party rounds, talking to everyone. She seemed to know everyone except Elizabeth and Raven. She spent quite a while talking to Raven. I could see that Raven had been fully assessed. Danae liked her!

Vince joined Steve and Georgia. They chatted animatedly as old friends.

After a half hour, Danae looked at her watch and then pulled Vince from a group conversation. They came to me.

"Is there a place we can talk in private?"

I led them to the TV room and closed the door.

Vince spoke. "I've had a good year in my venture capital firm. I plan on moving a great deal more money into the Foundation and believe it now needs full-time management. We are offering you a position as the CEO of the Colson Foundation. You will direct our further missionary efforts of encouraging scientists to investigate paranormal phenomena. Here is our formal offer."

I opened and scanned the letter. "This is generous. I need to discuss this with Phil Bracken before I reply."

"Of course, you should," said Vince. "I've talked to him as a courtesy. He said he would be reluctant to see you go. But, he wouldn't stand in your way."

This is a win-win situation. I get a new job, and Phil gets to tell Sam Perris of CharMed that I'm no longer with the law firm. Sam will think he won and got me fired.

"You can set up your office anywhere you like, as long as it's near an airport. The L.A. area is okay."

"You will report to me for most matters, added Danae. The first effort will be establishing research grants to various universities, like that with Dr. Montgomery. You will have other legal responsibilities. As far as we know, we have no more trials one on the horizon. We can talk details later. Let's get back to the celebration."

Soon, the catered dinner was served. It was quite a party.

After desert, Vince looked at Danae. "We have to leave for Palo Alto now."

After we had exchanged pleasantries, they left. I noticed that Danae's goodbye to Raven was warm. She had won Danae's approval.

The next morning, everyone was sleeping in. I awoke Raven and told her that we needed to go into town for breakfast in Rocky Butte. I need to talk to Agnes in Bob's cafe and say goodbye to the Sodastroms

At Bob's Cafe, somewhat to Raven's surprise, we sat on stools at the counter. Four rough-looking cowboys, wearing their cowboy hats, sitting in a booth, told Agnes something while she was taking their orders. She shrugged her shoulders, came over to us, carefully looking Raven over, and said, "What'll-y-have?"

"Two scrambled eggs." Raven added, "The Denver Omelet."

Agnes looked me straight in the eye and said, "Congratulations on creating Rocky Butte's first millionaires and putting the Sheriff in his place."

"Thanks, but that isn't exactly true. Their suit will be locked in appeals courts for years to come. The insurance companies will try to drag it out forever. The Sodastroms will not get a penny for years. People shouldn't try to hit them up for donations or grub stakes on mining ventures. They don't have any new money. Tell all the potential kidnappers of Ann and Ed that unless they want to hold captives for years, there will be no money for ransom."

"Really?" She sounded surprised.

"And, our law firm doesn't get paid from the settlement until the Sodastroms do. I'm not leaving here with a fat paycheck. I did not get rich off the Sodastroms' hard luck."

"Too bad. That's disappointing for the Sodastroms, I mean."

Agnes leaned over as if she was sharing a confidence with Raven. "The boys over there think you were the girl who beat up Chester Dawson at The Claim Jumper yesterday. Is that true?"

Raven lowered her head in mock embarrassment and replied in her fake southern accent, "I was at The Claim Jumper yesterday with one of my girl friends, and I saw those big cowboys scrabbling about something. How could somebody like little old me beat up a big cowboy? Well, I'll say."

"I'll tell them," replied Agnes.

As we got back in the car, I said to Raven, "You've created another legend for Rocky Butte. You're probably the biggest thing since Sasquatch.

We visited the Sodastroms briefly and returned to the ranch.

25

GLAMOROUS PRIMITIVE

Ten cars were in front of the lodge when we returned from Bob' cafe. Maids and workmen cleaned the main room.

Buster stood next to his suitcases and Sophia's trunk, talking to a small man dressed as a cowboy. When he saw us, he motioned for Raven and me to join them.

"Mr. Willard, meet Hank Wayne, the Manager of the Bar H Ranch. Hank, this is Raven Corbin."

"Mighty pleased to meet you. Has your stay here been to your likin?"

This guy is a real cowboy. He has a leathered face from years in the sun and his tan ends just above his eyebrows at his at his hat line

"It has been wonderful!" Raven nodded with a smile.

"It has been perfect for my witnesses and me. Having them in one place was a big plus."

"That pleases me greatly to hear. Mr. Cabot has allowed me to bring the Bar H Ranch staff back. They and the ranch are at your disposal until next weekend when other guests will arrive."

"I'll stay a few days to finish paperwork up with the County," said Elizabeth. "I'll take Ben up on his offer to give me riding lessons." She blushed as she added, "Ben said something about learning something called 'wrangling.'"

Hank smiled. "I reckon he has a reputation as a great wrangler."

Elizabeth turned to me, "I need to thank you. Catered dinners, fine champagne, clients who fly in Learjets, thirteen-million dollars, Raven as a companion, that's big time. I'm delighted I got to assist." She offered her hand.

"Thank you, It was a pleasure to work with you, even if we had to give up the usual two-hour two-martini lunches in our home office."

Buster walked up and shook my hand. "We'll be leaving now. We are going up the mountain for a few days of hiking."

"How can I say thank you for everything? You saved my life and let me concentrate on what I came here to do."

"It's part of the service. Here is the list of movies we've worked in that Raven requested."

"What's the name of the movie you'll be working on next?"

"It doesn't have a name yet. I'll send you tickets to the premier."

"I'll miss you," cried Sophia as she ran over to Raven and hugged her. They cried like long lost sisters.

"If this man ever gives you any trouble, let me know." She winked at me. Raven took a karate position, "Yes, we can double team on him."

Buster picked up his suitcases. Two of Hank's men picked up Sophia's trunk. We followed them to the porch. Buster whispered, "Sophia had something in her costume chest you might need. I put it in your desk." We said final goodbyes and walked back to the lodge.

Raven looked at me. "That's one more chapter closed in our lives."

That's truer than you know. I don't want to discuss Colson's letter until I have sorted out a bunch of things.

As we walked into the lodge, we met Hank.

Raven tugged on my arm. "Dave, can we stay two more days? We could go swimming and hiking. You promised me that sunset canoe ride."

"Good idea! I need idle time."

"I know just what you might fancy," said Hank. "There's a small cabin on the other side of the lake. It's very isolated with no electricity or cell service. It has indoor plumbing and a shower. An antique phone on the wall is connected to another phone in the lodge kitchen for calling room service. We call the place glamorous primitive.

After lunch we met Ben at the dock on the lake.

"The cabin is prepared for you. It's only a ten-minute boat ride. I towed the canoe over there earlier when I took the maids to dust the place."

Raven climbed into the skiff. "This is exciting! It's like we are going to be stranded on a desert island."

With room service.

As we got underway, Ben said, "Champagne, wine, and beer are in the icebox on the porch. What time should we bring dinner?"

I looked at Raven. "Six-thirty? That will give us time for dinner and that sunset canoe ride."

Raven nodded her head.

"Someone will bring you a breakfast hamper and leave it on the dock in the morning. What time would you like it dropped off?"

Raven spoke up, "About eight. We have a full day ahead of us tomorrow."

I was reading a book while sitting in a rocking chair on the cabin porch when the screen door slammed. Raven walked out wearing a flowered dress.

"You look beautiful! That's dressy for camping in a primitive cabin. I like the way you've done your hair."

"They don't have hair dryers in glamorous primitive accommodations. I had to improvise."

"I wanted to get dressed for dinner. This is a special occasion."

"I'm sorry I didn't bring my tux."

"Cowboy style jeans with your pearl buttoned shirt are just fine." She gave me a big kiss.

"Why don't you open one of those bottles of Champaign, I saw in the ice-box."

We sat in the rocking chairs holding hands and talking. After a while, Raven looked at me. "I thought we'd hurry back to CrystalSky to catch up on your glider flying."

"That's not a priority now. The time-travel to World War I and dealing with those emotions changed all that. I used to need to fly. It was a compulsion."

Raven laughed. "Really? I never noticed that."

"I was trying to solve an old problem by winning the Diamond Soaring Badge. That was to make up for not being awarded the World War One flying medal, the Blue Max. Now that has been understood, I don't need to pursue that goal.

My trust of women issues were resolved when I saw the woman in the white hat in the same era."

Rave frowned. "I hope you will still invite me to your desert home. I'd hate to see you sell that."

"No plans to sell that. But, now I have new options."

That's true. It's time to discuss Colson's job offer.

I reached into the back of my book and produced Colson's letter. "This is one of my options."

Raven read it with astonishment and asked, "What does this mean?"

"This will be a new career for me. It'll change my life plan. It means I can work at home. No more extended stays away from home doing trial work. I will deal with academics interested in extending science rather than lawyers trying to generate billable hours. It means I can settle down and live someplace without long absences."

She looked at the letter again. "I've no Idea how much lawyers earn. By school teacher's standard, this is a lot of money."

"For me, it's a raise. It's also a rebirth. I'm making big decisions and changes in my life, and I want you to be part of them.

"Please stand up a second."

I dropped to one knee and held her hand.

She looked surprised and said, "Oh my God, he's doing the down on one knee thing!"

The golden light of the late afternoon sun made her face and hair glow.

"Will you marry me?"

"Yes! Yes! Yes! Or more succinctly, Yes." She pulled me up and threw her arms around my neck, kissed me for a long time and then tipped her head back, looked me in the eyes and said, "That means yes–maybe I should clarify that, Yes, Yes."

I pulled the theatrical prop fake diamond ring Buster left from my pocket. I slid it on her finger.

"That's the biggest diamond ring I've ever seen! Who are you? What did you do with Dave Willard?"

"Let's sit." She looked about to faint.

"And its size is adjustable." I turned her hand over to show the underside of the ring. "See you can squeeze these two bands to make it fit. There is no place in Rocky Butte to buy a ring. Sophia had this in her costume jewelry collection. Buster gave it to me, as he said, 'in case of emergency.' We will shop for a real ring when we get back to L.A.."

"I will never give this back! At least until I show it to all my friends."

She pulled me to my feet and kissed me. "What was I was going to tell you? Oh, I remember. Yes!

She turned and picked up the Champagne bottle and filled our flutes. She stepped back and raised her glass to click mine and said in her most sophisticated voice. "I believe the occasion deserves a proper answer: Yes."

26

THE UNION

I held the stern of the canoe on the beach as she gingerly climbed in. "Sit facing me on the bottom of the bow. Take the bottle of brandy and plastic cups. I learned long ago not to bring glasses in boats. Scars on the soles of my feet prove it."

After pushing the canoe free of the beach, I scrambled into the stern. She stroked a wooden rib of the canoe. "This is marvelous. These ribs were bent so perfectly. The varnished wood makes it classic. Those little wicker seats are cute. It's tippy though. They should have a sign in here that says, 'No Dancing Allowed.'"

I kneeled on the bottom and paddled. She trailed one hand in the water and admired the ring on her other hand.

"This is the happiest day of my life! Everything's perfect!".

A hundred yard from shore I stopped paddling and turned the canoe sideways so we both could enjoy the sunset. A golden glow lit the few cumulous clouds left over from the day.

She poured two generous cups of brandy.

"To us!" She raised her cup in a toast as we both sat on the bottom of the canoe.

"To our bountiful future," I toasted in reply. The sun dipped lower.

Raven filled our cups.

"A toast!" I said, rising to sit on the thin wicker seat. "To you, love of my life! My guiding spirit through a most important period of change in my life!"

I held the gunwale of the canoe with one hand and shakily stood up.

"To your love and companionship, I will cherish the rest of my days."

The canoe rocked from side-to-side as I tried to steady it.

Raven stood and held up her cup.

I desperately tried to steady the canoe's rocking.

"And to you, love of my life who compliments me and has expanded my horizon and taught me the delight of adventure. I look forward to sharing my life with you.

The canoe rolled and water flooded in. The boat started to capsize. I laughed, and Raven screamed as we tumbled into the water.

I came up first, grabbed the boat gunwale and looked for. Raven. Her hand with the engagement ring broke the water and grabbed the canoe gunwall. She surfaced and shook her wet hair out of her eyes. She still had her cup in her hand.

"I'd better rescue the brandy." I swam to it. Raven retrieved my cup.

She rested her elbow on the side of the flooded canoe, took both cups and poured out the water.

"Here, more brandy."

I filled the cups. We both drank and looked each other in the eyes, treaded water and watched the sunset.

She shook wet hair out of her eyes "What do we do now?"

I sipped my brandy. "We should get married?"

Raven took my hand. "I think we just did."

The clerk said, "That will be thirty-five dollars."

I handed her bills. Raven stood next to me holding my arm.

"Judge Cartwright can perform the ceremony during his noon recess."

"No thank you, we have other arrangements."

We walked from the County Clerk's Office to the hall and met Steve and Georgia who beamed with huge smiles.

Steve shook my hand. "You guys believe in long engagements. What's it been? Fourteen hours? Raven is anyone else invited to the wedding?"

"I called my best friend Elise this morning to give her the news. She insisted on flying up from L.A. for the ceremony. Ben said he'd pick her up at eight o'clock tomorrow morning in Sacramento."

"How about you, Dave?"

"I have asked my associate, Elizabeth to be my 'Best Person.' She is bringing Ben as a date."

Georgia hugged Raven and looked at me. "We will take care of all the plans for a noon wedding tomorrow. Okay? Everyone will be here by then."

I looked at Raven. She nodded. Her eyes were wide open.

"Dave, you go with Steve. He has a bachelor party planned."

She took Raven by the hand. "You come with me. We have shopping to do. Everyone, we will get together just before noon tomorrow at the ceremonial site."

As they walked away, I said to Steve, "Bachelor party?"

"I hope it won't disappoint you. It will be a ceremony in a sweat lodge. It's a purification thing. Okay?"

"Yes, I need to get rid of the lawyer energy left over from the trial."

The next morning, Steve drove Elizabeth and me up the mountain on a dirt road that dead-ended in small parking lot. We followed a path for a short walk to a cliff with a view of the pine-filled valley.

Steve said, "Sit here on this log while I prepare the energy of the circle for the ceremony. The circle is on the other side of those trees. A local tribe used it for sacred ceremonies a a long time ago. I'll let you know when it's ready."Elizabeth, dressed in a flowing black dress, looked at me. "A Beverly Hills lawyer dressed like this for his wedding? Are those new Levis? The black pearl-buttoned shirt is a nice touch. I have never seen you in a hat."

"Hank at the Dude Ranch gave me this Stetson. They have an inventory of hats for visitors."

Back at Steve and Georgia's home, Georgia and Elise helped Raven get into her white wedding dress. As Raven did her makeup, they nervously chatted.

Georgia was fixing Ravens hem.

Elise fluffed Raven's hair, "You look beautiful! Where in the world did you get that lovely bridal dress?"

"Georgia took me to a local dressmaker who made this for another woman who eloped and never picked it up. It was almost a perfect fit. It was pure magic it was there."

Georgia made a wry smile but didn't look up.

After they got into Georgia's car and began the drive, Georgia said, "Raven, you have a strange vibration coming off your body. This feels like more than the usual bride's jitters. Is everything all right? Are you getting second thoughts about getting married?"

"No, nothing like that. I have a feeling that I am already married to someone else. I feel great joy somehow mixed with doubt, almost guilt."

Georgia stared at Raven with a stern expression. "Did you forget to tell us this is your second marriage? Are you divorced?"

Raven waved her hand. "No, I'm single.

Elise added, "I've been picking up that energy. I've known you a long time. You only radiate that when something is wrong."

Georgia gave Raven a long piercing look. "I got it. I see the pictures. We will sort this out when we get to the ceremonial site."

After they had parked the car next to Steve's, they saw tracks on a path leading into the woods. Georgia took a second path to a small clearing. Georgia sat Raven on a stump. "Have you heard Dave, Candice, and Steve talking about how time and space are only an illusion."

"Yes, but in meant nothing to me."

"I'm picking up pictures from you. Your attention is in another space and time."

"I feel it too. You aren't even here," said Elise. "What's going on?"

Georgia put her hand on Raven's shoulder "Tell me what you are feeling and what visions you are seeing."

"I see myself in what must be another lifetime, feeling great joy about my pending marriage. I am getting ready for the ceremony."

"Yes, I can see the pictures." Georgia burst into a big smile.

"A voice inside me today is saying, 'I'm already married. I can't get married to Dave.'"

Georgia stared at Raven and then asked, "Does the groom seem familiar?"

"He's dressed in a medieval outfit."

"Where are you?"

"It looks like an ancient church."

"What date is it?"

"I get the idea it was fifteen-hundred something."

"Does he seem familiar?" coached Georgia. "Concentrate on the groom. Do you know him?"

Raven thought a while and then said, "Oh my God! It's Dave in a medieval life. He was my husband!"

"Yippee!" said Georgia, "You got it!"

"What does it mean?" asked Raven.

"It's okay to marry Dave again. There is unfinished business with him from that lifetime. I'm sure it's a happy, loving business.

"Are you ready to get married to Dave again?"

"Oh, yes! Now, it feels right."

"Three cheers!" Said Elise. "You had me scared." She gave Raven a big hug. "Girl, you were psychically spying on the sixteenth century."

Georgia stood. "Good! I'll check if everything is ready. I'll be right back."

Raven sat with her eyes closed and glowed with love and excitement.

"That's more like it." Elise held her hand.

"It is time." Raven opened her eyes. Georgia motioned for her to come

❋

Elise lead Raven to the center of the circle from the north side. Steve led me, follow by Elizabeth from the south. A faint blue glow of energy formed at the center of the circle as we approached.

As I stepped into the circle part of the blue energy formed a bubble around me. From the inside, I could see a myriad of golden flecks in the light swirling as the bubble pulsed with my heartbeat. I felt an enormous joy and love.

Raven was also inside another shimmering bubble pulsing with her heartbeat. She was beautiful and serene.

Steve stood with eyes closed and hands spread and raised. "Please join hands."

The bubbles came together as we joined hands. Raven had taken off her 'engagement ring.'

Steve still held up his hands. "Raven and Dave have something to say for all to hear."

"Raven, I promise my unconditional love and commitment for this lifetime."

"Dave, I promise my unconditional love and commitment for this lifetime."

Steve produced two wedding bands from his pocket and handed them to us. "You may exchange rings to signify this commitment."

"I now pronounce you 'Husband and Wife.'" When I kissed Raven the golden fog dissolved into our bodies.

Elise, Georgia, and Elizabeth joined us, and everyone shared hugs.

Ben, who was standing under a pine tree called, "Over here! The reception is under this tree! I have champagne in a cooler and Hank sent a mini banquet." He had set up a folding table laden with a buffet.

As I took Raven's hand, She looked into my eyes. "Earlier today I was feeling uncertain about getting married. Something was wrong. I was already married. Georgia helped me discover that I had been married to you six-hundred years ago. She said it would be okay to marry you again."

I squeezed her hand. "I have sensed there was a bond with you since first we met. Our love has no bounds in space-time."

Raven stepped back. "Now I understand. For our love, space and time are only an illusion."

ACKNOWLEDGMENTS

I thank Russel Targ for his patience and guidance when I was writing *Science, Remote Viewing. and ESP.* That thesis provided the conceptual framework for this story

I thank my fellow writers, and Paula Cizmar at Rough Writers for their support and comments. Roxane Broderick's careful final editing amazed me. And special thanks to Heather UpChurch for her inspired cover design.

ABOUT THE AUTHOR

Ken Renshaw had a career as a scientist designing and marketing communication satellites to space communication companies.

A few years ago, Ken Renshaw took a course in Remote Viewing from Russel Targ one of the pioneers in the field, at the Esalen Institute in Big Sur. He was surprised at how easy it was to use clairvoyant abilities. His background as a scientist compelled him to develop a scientific theory of how it works.

Many people debunk psychic phenomena such as Remote Viewing and ESP because of a lack of scientific support. Ken Renshaw's book, *Science, Remote Viewing and ESP*, provides a complete theory of how Remote Viewing and clairvoyance work in terms of Modern Physics and Biology.

The book explains everything in lay terms. Anyone with high school mathematics can understand the science behind the theory and why it works. Ken Renshaw's book has been praised by readers for presenting the subject in simple terms.

He wrote the novel, *The Trial of the Psychic Spy*, to illustrate how clairvoyance can occur in everyday life.